"*The Misheard World* is riveting, weird, unpredictable, and magnificent. This is Aliya Whiteley at her inimitable best."

Oliver K. Langmead, author of *Calypso*

"Each sentence does more work than you expect, each image cuts deeper than it first appears. A stunning achievement."

Helen Marshall, author of
The Lady, the Tiger and the Girl Who Loved Death

"Artfully woven and humming with the power and possibilities of the spoken word, *The Misheard World* confirms Aliya Whiteley as one of our most original and exciting writers. I loved this book."

E. J. Swift, author of *The Coral Bones*

"Deftly conjures an alien world that echoes our own, or perhaps it's the other way around… Whiteley never puts a foot wrong, and *The Misheard World* is another triumph to add to her list of many."

Tim Major, author of *Snakeskins*

Praise for
THREE EIGHT ONE

"A wonderfully alienating experience."

SFX, five star review

"A puzzle box full of delights, perils and strange
wonders. Haunting."

Mike Carey

"Brilliant in its playful inventiveness."

The FT

"An exquisitely crafted, beautifully realized voyage
of discovery."

E. J. Swift

"A quirky, unsettling work from
one of the most original writers of
speculative fiction in Britain today."

The Guardian

"Funny and thoughtful, frightening and joyful.
I already want to go back."

Matt Hill

Praise for
SKYWARD INN

"A melancholy and compellingly weird
tale of identity in crisis."

SFX

"Intense and consuming writing, constantly
challenging expectations."

Adrian Tchaikovsky

"A unique work of literary and
speculative excellence."

SciFiNow

"One of the most original and provocative voices in
contemporary science fiction."

Nina Allan

"Whiteley's trademark subtle surrealism shines."

Publishers Weekly

"Whiteley takes the reader on a
cryptic journey of trust, identity and
knowing your place in the world."

Starburst Magazine

THE
MISHEARD
WORLD

Also by Aliya Whiteley

The Beauty
The Loosening Skin
Skein Island
Greensmith
Skyward Inn
Three Eight One

ALIYA WHITELEY

THE MISHEARD WORLD

SOLARIS

First published 2026 by Solaris
an imprint of Rebellion Publishing Ltd,
Riverside House, Osney Mead,
Oxford OX2 0ES, UK

www.solarisbooks.com

ISBN: 978-1-83786-691-5

10 9 8 7 6 5 4 3 2 1

A CIP catalogue record for this book is available from
the British Library.

Designed & typeset by Rebellion Publishing

Printed in the United Kingdom

For Tim Stretton
Thank you

BOOK ONE
CRAG

CHAPTER ONE

WE WERE CALLED to the dock to collect a box.

It was the end of spring, the beginning of summer, the time that lay between the two, and cold air poured down from the mountains, over the stone of Crag. The peaks behind us formed an impassable barrier from all sides except that of the water. The only way to reach us was by boat, and we had eyes upon Lake Haspen at all times. There could be no shock tactic for the enemy and yet, that morning, we were all surprised by the delivery.

The box was taller and wider than a normal man. From a length of rope around its middle hung a creamy-white tag of expensive card that caught my eye. I was not close enough to read the message written upon it.

"Mondegreen," whispered Pappas, on my right.

Mondegreen was as famous as a legend and as loved as a hero, by both sides alike. But when war broke out he had chosen north over south: them above us. How could he have committed such a betrayal? Beyond that act, his unique reputation for spycraft made him a prize. He had been the famous entertainer, performing impossible feats, before the war. He could read minds, breathe fire, balance on wires strung between the highest buildings, make objects appear and disappear. He could affect emotions, alter perceptions, and make people see things that weren't real. He was said to be the finest of all storytellers. I didn't think we would ever catch him. It was impossible, surely? Mondegreen could not be shut into a box.

"Take it inside," said the officer, and I snatched my eyes away from the tag. Pappas put his hands on the box and I followed suit. It took half a dozen of us to manoeuvre it on to the wheeled trolley we used for hauling supplies. I was next to no help throughout, being a poor pick for this duty: slim, weak in the upper arms, no matter how many push ups I attempted. I tried my best. The planks were unplaned, and badly nailed together. I received a splinter for my troubles. The pain of it brought clarity. I thought to myself: *If we hold him inside this box, transport him cruelly and to amuse ourselves, we are as bad as they are*, and I hated the world a little more.

It seemed so unlikely that any man was inside. No sound

was made throughout our awkward handling. There were no slits or gaps in the wood. Three small airholes had been drilled in a triangular formation, low down, at the base.

As we took the box through the main gate I glanced behind me, and saw the ferry setting sail back to Stravatch, across the lake, moving slowly, seeming reluctant to return. Stravatch was under threat; the forces of the north had reached the hills behind the town a week earlier, but were yet few in number and had not moved upon it. I wished I was there, ready to fight. I was not grateful to have been assigned guard duty, unlike others. How could I find who was to blame for this war, from inside the safety of these walls? I needed someone to hate. But most of those captured and imprisoned in Crag had lost their will to fight before they even arrived; and their first view of the imposing north wall of the prison, unscalable, hewn from the rock face, knocked resistance from the rest. It was a monumental, intimidating sight. I could not find it in myself to think them accountable, not when the fight had left them so utterly.

We steered the trolley through the gate, and it closed behind us. The vast metal bars were slammed across, and the outside world was dismissed once more. Nothing mattered within but the rules. Once we reached the centre of the courtyard we unloaded the box from the trolley, and stood to attention close by.

I wanted to see him for myself.

The clock, high in the west tower, ticked towards ten, and Warden Beck strolled with deliberate ease through the main arch, clean and straight in his best uniform, the black high collar barely faded. No doubt he had watched the arrival of the box from his office window. He was a man of obsessive punctuality, with an intense and puritanical sense of flair, and he wielded it to the fullest as he crossed the courtyard, hands behind his back, chin in the air. He approached the box and read the tag. Frowned.

"A present from The Allynx Syld," he said, to himself, to the courtyard. "She hopes it brings us happiness, as a presentiment of a swing towards better times. Let us open it."

Pappas fetched a crowbar and set to work with his strong shoulders and meaty hands. He soon forced a creaking gap between two planks. He stepped back, examined the wood, then reapplied the crowbar, and this time the wood groaned and gave up. The box broke, and the sides fell away to reveal the man inside.

I knew him immediately.

He was there, really there, his dark hair loose over hunched shoulders. Was this the great performer of our time? He smelled, he cowered. Of course; he had been caged like an animal. I knew him even though I had not yet seen his face. It was all in the line of the body, the tension and the poise that this barbaric act of transportation could not erase.

"This is not Mondegreen," said Warden Beck, slowly.

Silence.

"This cannot be him."

I watched the man tremble, his muscles straining, as he lifted his face, his eyes closed against the light. He had not aged, to me. For a moment I was twelve years old again, slipping away from my duties to admire the way he did not seem quite of this world.

"Is this the man?" said Warden Beck, and I could not help myself.

I said, "Yes. This is Mondegreen."

The warden's eyes swung to me. I had never spoken to him before. My plan had always been to stay low, be unnoticed, dream my dreams of finding justice without the interference of military authority.

"You're sure?"

"Sir, I've seen him before," I said. "I watched him perform. Before the chasm."

"And you're certain? This is one and the same?"

I thought of his lightness, his balance. The tricks he had performed, the tightrope he had walked, and the rich people clapping and cheering, and talking of impossibilities made real. At the end he had simply vanished from the rope, leaving a pinkish cloud dispersing, and somehow the scent of a warm wood fire in the air. And he had left me with a gift: a gift I still cherished.

I waited.

"Well?"

"Sir, I'm certain," I said, and Mondegreen was led away, into Crag, while the warden cut free the tag to keep. I helped to clean up the remains of the box, stacking the wood in the corner of the courtyard, wondering how such a flimsy construction had managed to imprison a legend.

CHAPTER TWO

"YOU ARE ELIZE Janview."

I stood to attention before the imposing polished desk. Warden Beck sat behind it with his usual immaculate posture, but he had changed into one of his working uniforms since that morning, and the remains of his lunch were on a silver tray, pushed to the far side of the desk. Crusts of bread, the rind of a strong local cheese that I didn't care for; on the southern coast, where I had been born, the flavours were more delicate. I could see the note that had swung from the box containing Mondegreen, now tucked under the rim of the tray.

"Speak up," said the warden, but gently. He was not known as a tyrannical man. His eyes were still on the thin file that I assumed held my military record to date. I had never thought to be present in his office at all, with only six months left to go of my service. It was a smaller room than I had expected, and uncluttered. Faded paintings in simple frames hung from the wall behind the door. One small shelf of a handful of books was mounted behind his head, in my line of vision. An insipid carpet lay under the legs of the desk, and a thin fire burned in the grate.

"Yes, sir."

"You are nearly twenty-four years old."

"Yes, sir."

"You signed up at sixteen. One of the youngest, back at the start of the war."

I did not reply to that.

He closed the file and leaned forward, putting his elbows on the desk, his hands clasped in front of him. "Janview," he said. "What are you doing here?"

There were a number of ways to take that question. "I am committed to seeing the south through its time of need, sir."

"Even though that has led you to eight years of this duty? Didn't you sign up for more? For combat? Action? Glory, even?" His gaze dimmed, and I read in his eyes the lines of his own memories, from when he had been a young soldier steeped in honour. In earlier times he was a grunt, like us: Pappas had told me, one night, between dice throws. At the Mellik clash—a rare engagement between north and south back then, forty years in the past—he took on an emplacement, swept it clean. Fifteen of them. And every shot honourable, through the heart or head. No suffering.

Looking at his severe, aging face at that moment, I could see it: a belief in heroic actions, in personal victory. The question came to me—why had he not railed against the transportation of Mondegreen in such a demeaning way? If he truly was a man of honour, he could never have borne such a sight. But then it came to me that I had not publicly registered my objection either, and I was not about to. The degradation of the soul was a never-ending business, in this place. We were all losers.

"Well?"

"I am... not content, sir," I said. "I requested front line duty, but found nothing there but waiting." I had spent three years sitting a few miles outside Stravatch without once getting close to an enemy. It had been a strange stalemate since Droad, as if neither side wished to act, but I had needed to look a foe in the face, to try to see a reason there for what happened. Eventually I had requested a transfer to Crag, to at least have the chance to examine those from the north who had been captured during the very few skirmishes, further west.

"I can see you are like me. You must tell the truth, or suffer. And that suits my needs right now. So..." He cleared his throat, lowered his voice. "You lived in Droad. Your admission documents list the Mutuality as your address. You were too young to be government staff, surely?"

"My mother worked in the kitchens," I said. I did not elaborate. It was a strange moment, to have my personal pain spoken aloud. He was astute, watching my face. He had plans for me; I saw it clearly, and could not begin to guess at their nature. That roused a rebellious streak in me I had long thought conquered. I did not reply. I lifted my chin, and stared past him, and his cherished books, to the heavy grey curtains that had been tied back from the window—the only window I had seen in years that was not covered by thick iron bars.

"You can keep secrets too, I see. Perfect. I need you to keep some more, for the good of the south. Can you do that?"

Finally, a question I could answer well, and easily. "I can, sir."

"Excellent. Here is the situation. The most distinguished and elusive Mondegreen is going to have a visitor. A series of interviews has been arranged. You will sit in, and observe. They will talk of places and events you will know, such as Droad, and the chasm it became. Of customs and beliefs, and theories." He waved one hand in the air. "Life, and so on. They'll talk of life. You will listen, and report back. Do you understand?"

"No, sir."

My reply raised a small smile from him. "Has anyone ever told you that too much honesty is not necessarily a good thing?"

The words of my long-dead tutor, Master Fider, came to mind. Another victim of Droad. *Think before you speak, and do not always speak what you think.* "They have, sir."

"In this case, they were wrong. You will report everything that is said between the visitor and prisoner. You will leave nothing out, including your own impressions. But I must stress—you hold no rank above observer. It is your ability to be unremarkable, as well as your honesty and your background, that makes you so well suited for this task. You will be nameless and faceless. This is particularly necessary when you sit in Mondegreen's presence. He is famous for his charm; he will be under orders not to speak to you directly, or look at you. If he does, he will be severely punished. I need you to be... invisible. As invisible as you've been to me for the past eight years."

I shifted my weight, feeling a discomfort I could not name. It was as if something within Crag had appeared, a shadow over the rock itself, poised to blot me out.

"You have a question?" said Beck. "Ask it. Anything may be spoken between us relating to this task. Do you believe that?"

"Who is to be the visitor?"

I dreaded the answer. I had heard rumours of a new kind of warfare, where tortures were inflicted upon the enemy to gain an advantage. *Please,* I thought, *not that: to watch Mondegreen suffer.*

"Here," he said. He slipped the note from the tray, and passed it to me. I had been right about the quality of the paper. It was thick, smooth and creamy, under my fingers.

To Warden Beck and the good soldiers of the Crag,
   Please find enclosed a present that I hope will bring us all happiness. He is, I believe, the key to the end of this conflict. I follow shortly, to unlock him.
   From your dear friend and most loyal colleague
   The Allynx Syld

This was a name I knew. The lady took her title from the legendary big cat of the far north to whom she was inextricably linked: the Allynx, beautiful and cruel and beyond the concerns of humanity. I had even stood in her presence, once. The Syld had been a rare visitor to Droad, giving all she met her fine smile and pleasant conversation—until the strike that had wiped that city from the land, and created the chasm. That attack had changed her from the socialite she had been. She had sided with us, speaking openly against the barbarism of the north even though Avock, high in the mountains, was said to have been her place of birth. She began to speak out, and to use her talents to challenge high-ranking enemies as if it was sport.

"You worry as to the form of interview?" I realised he had read my mind easily. He was not wrong; I was transparent,

unable to keep my thoughts from my face. A bright delight—
that was what my mother had used to call my countenance.
I wondered if she would think me much changed if she saw
me now. "Don't be concerned. You have only to wait until the
morning to find your answers, and to be reassured, since my
word will not do. You'll be summoned."

An Allynx, locked in a small room with her prey. And I was
to stand back and watch her game in action.

He looked me up and down, and I thought I detected
something unexpected in his tone, a cadence almost
sympathetic, as he said, "There are many ways to be a hero,
and not all of them involve death. Everyone is given their
moment to serve their country; and this, Elize Janview, is
yours."

CHAPTER THREE

WHEN EVERYONE HAS a story of loss to tell, nothing is worthy of the grand title of tragedy. Each tale contributes only to a mound of sadness: heaped, unclimbable, the stories slowly bleeding into each other until they are impossible to tell apart. Brother, sister, father, daughter. Mother. Piled high, the mound getting bigger. I had no wish to add to it, so I did not talk about my personal losses every night, in the main hall, by the glow of the stone hearth. For some, the repetition of the names of the victims of this war were all they lived for. They grew tiresome in their desire to hear the names aloud. I avoided them, when I could.

There were others who felt as I did, and we congregated at the back of the long room, by the stack of empty bowls on the trestle tables and the tureen of daily soup. We accepted the distance from the fire, the freezing fingers of the shadows creeping down the thick walls and into our uniforms, as the price for not speaking of that pile of the dead. We were alive, and to prove it, we gambled.

We placed bets on anything. Two ants on the floor, or two drops of beer running down the side of a cup. The subjects could just as easily be momentous: when will the war end? Pick a date. Which town will they use the weapon on next? Mark it on a map. No subject was sacred.

Imberley was the keenest of gamblers, but I suspected her motive was different. I could see desperation in her; she wanted to believe in luck so badly, and then to find it on her side. When we had taken bets on who would die first, she had named me. Later, on duty together, I had asked her why, since I already had a reputation for avoiding conflict in our small group. I never took part in the wrestling bouts, and had not perfected the use of any weapon. How should I ever find my way into combat?

Not in battle, she had said. *But I think you might...*

She mimed a noose, her tongue lolling. I should have hated her for that, but somehow it prompted the opposite emotion, and I enjoyed the thought that she had observed me, made a judgement. It also amused me that her judgement was wrong. I never would have done such a thing, not if I lived to be a thousand years old. My life had a purpose she could not have begun to guess at. My mother, Fider, and everyone who had been obliterated at Droad, were relying on me to make sure something so terrible never happened again. A ridiculous goal, but I would live for it.

"Your turn to start," said Pappas, the night of Mondegreen's arrival, and I rolled the die. Three. It was the most basic of games, but it worked as well as any other, at the end of long shifts.

"Hah!" he said, and rolled a five to claim a wrap of hot pepper from me. I checked the pouch I kept inside my jacket. Two wraps left, then my allowance for the week would be squandered once more, and the soup would be beyond bland.

I loved to gamble, but I was no good at it. I had an idea that Pappas cheated, too, but I couldn't see how it was done and wouldn't have dared to accuse him. He was from the west: the cold desert land. His paler skin was lined with the marks of a hard life, and he was one of the oldest still serving, having signed back up twice. But he exercised and took care of himself, the white stubble on his head and chin shaved regularly to the nub. He claimed to have been one of the elite forces who infiltrated the Dhargens—a great victory for us—and to have escaped by sledding down the mountainside. I didn't believe that for a moment. Still, he laughed often and loudly and was good company, even if he did scare me and take all my hot pepper.

"Again?" he said.

"Why not?" I took up the die and blew on it, then whipped back my hand to deliver it, with style, to the waiting table. Two. Imberley and Tommo, sitting on either side of me, sighed.

Pappas smiled. He took up the die and slammed it down without ceremony. Six. I handed over another wrap.

"One left," I said. "I'm out."

"Then let's bet on something else."

"Like what?" said Imberley.

Pappas shrugged. "Like how long it'll take Mondegreen to escape."

Tommo's eyes widened. "But nobody escapes Crag," he said. He was dark, tall, very young, and keen to find invulnerability, or goodness, or bravery—some unassailable quality—in his existence. I liked him very much, and had named him as the one who would die first.

"Didn't that commander from the far north make it outside the walls?" mused Pappas.

"He was shot from the battlement before he got twenty paces! I saw it myself."

"Still, it technically counts as an escape," said Imberley, and we all laughed at Tommo's outraged expression. He was a delight to tease.

Pappas took out his little notepad and pencil, always on hand for such wagers, and started to make notes. "I'll put Tommo down as a 'never' for Mondegreen's escape, then. Imbie?"

"In the next three days," she said, very seriously.

"He's only just arrived!" Pappas protested.

She grimaced, then said, softly, "He's a legend."

"I don't care if he can sprout wings and take off—he still needs to know the layout, find a gap in the routines, or we'll just shoot him down..." Pappas hummed, then said, "Thirty days, I reckon. Thirty to forty."

"Impossible!" Tommo protested.

"Jan?" said Imberley, fixing me with her direct gaze. "You're the only one who's seen him in action. Give us some insight."

I thought back over my memory of him, and tried to sort out what I could say. I would not explain myself, my mother, our circumstances. No mention of the dead here. What, then? "He's a brilliant performer. He... was the centre of a crowd, and he was in finery. A suit, and heeled shoes, and jewels in his earlobes. He smelled of oranges."

"You got close enough to *smell* him?"

"I was young. Good at being unseen." I had been carrying a tray of pastries, for the Mutuality guests to enjoy. That simple act had allowed me to circulate freely, to be accepted without comment. "He told stories, did tricks. Said outrageous things that made no sense—he lived up to his title. The Misheard Word. I wasn't sure I heard him right. And he had the quickest hands, too. Everyone laughed. Then he was up on a rope." In what order had it all happened? I couldn't recall. "He was there, somehow, suddenly, high above us. And then he was gone."

"Gone where?" breathed Tommo.

"I don't know. Nobody knew. But everyone in the place was missing a coin."

Pappas laughed, a startled sound. "What? A coin? Every single person?"

I nodded. "It was amazing. The most amazing thing I was ever part of. And I—"

"And you what?"

I had gone too far. It came back to me clearly, that moment, when I realised I was the only one not missing a coin, and that I had gained something instead: a bag of coins, tucked away in my pocket. It had been enough to pay for a first lesson with Master Fider, the private tutor to the Mutuality children, and I had been beyond fortunate; that one lesson had been enough to persuade Fider to take me on for free. He had seen potential in me, and I had grabbed that chance to learn, to search for meaning. Mondegreen's generosity that day had changed my life, given me the means to feed my voracious appetite for knowledge of the world we lived in.

"I—I, too, was astonished. I couldn't even begin to see how it was done. I had my eyes on him the whole time, through all his tricks."

That much was true. I had been unable to stop looking at him. How wondrous he had been, bigger and better than anyone I'd seen before, wearing his own reputation like a gem-studded cloak. Already famous, and infinitely easy to forgive; nobody in the crowd bemoaned the loss of a single coin. Why would they? It was an honour to have him take it. And then, at the end of the night, as the orchestra finished their last song, a black cloud had appeared over the ballroom and a bolt of lightning had zapped out, causing everyone's hair to stand on end. How could that be? But that was my memory. I described it to Pappas, Imberley and Tommo, careful to make the setting sound like a village square instead of the grand Mutuality. I wished to keep my connection to the north, as part of that experiment for both sides to live together, to myself. I talked of the gasps, the hands reaching up high.

"Unbelievable," said Imberley.

"Sounds like you saw him in his youth," said Pappas.

"I was a child," I agreed. "And he was…"

"What?"

There were many things I could have said. Handsome. Surprising. Dazzling. Free. He had been that unique thing— loved by all. I thought he had a strong liking of Droad. I saw him there often. But when the time came, he picked the north. I felt that he was, in some way to me personally, a traitor. Yes, he was a traitor.

"He was tall," I said.

"Thanks, Janview, for that stunning insight," said Imberley. "Truly eloquent. Tall. Please, gift us with more of your sweet phrases and tell us when you think the tall man will escape?"

My answer was partly due to my inability to reconcile the broken man, delivered in a box to our doorstep, to the figure I remembered. "Never," I said.

"See?" said Tommo. "Like I said. Nobody escapes Crag."

"At some point," said Imberley, "this war will end, and this place will go back to being a historical remnant of all our fights long past, over the centuries. It may not seem like it, but that is the way of all wars."

"Until the next starts," I said. "All right, then. Not in my lifetime. How's that?"

"Well, now," she said, with the flicker of a thin-lipped smile. "Fair enough. That's a different thing altogether, isn't it? A very different thing." She winked at me, and I opened my mouth to say—what? What on earth could I have said to put her, put anyone, in their place?

"Janview!"

The shout echoed across the main hall. Everyone fell silent, even those sharing their sadnesses, and watched Captain Shird, small and silvery like a fish, glide through the main hall. I shrank, and Tommo poked me in the side until I got to my feet, and stood to attention. The movement attracted her steely gaze. It seemed to me she thrived on precision, on alacrity. The weight of the day-to-day running of the defence of Crag was perhaps made bearable that way.

"Captain."

She looked me up and down, and I knew she found me wanting. "Report to the pinnacle after breakfast tomorrow."

"Yes, captain."

She said, "Don't let me down, Janview." Then surveyed the table. I saw her eyes rest on the die. "Fate is a foolish comfort," she said. It was an old expression. I knew the usual reply, but it was Pappas who spoke it aloud.

"Good deeds line the finest beds."

Shird smiled, rubbed her upper lip with the back of her hand. When she dropped her arm, her smile was gone. She left as swiftly as she had arrived.

Pappas whistled. "Requested for duty in the pinnacle." We all knew who the occupant of the most secure room in Crag would be. I couldn't risk replying, knowing my words would give away my nerves.

Tommo said, "What kind of assignment makes an errand-runner of Captain Shird?"

Imberley murmured, "Tommo, you're not as stupid as I thought. Janview, be careful. Keep your head down, and your mouth shut."

"Now that," I said, "won't be a problem."

They laughed, and we called quits on the evening. These were my friends, mainly because they never asked to be my confidantes. We knew the rules of the game too well for that. Everyone might have a story to tell, but whatever turn mine was about to take would remain my business alone.

CHAPTER FOUR

SHE WAS OLDER, to my eyes, but not lessened by it. She wore a plain grey dress, not the finery that she was known to favour. I remember how, once, I was dazzled by her: her jewels and sweeping trains, and the famed pure white fur she wore around her shoulders; her detached, yet amused expression; that cool gaze of hers that swept over the ballroom in Droad Mutuality. That same look now sized up the current situation, took me in, and identified me as an underling, but I did not feel belittled. She beckoned me closer, and I went to her.

"Your name?"

Of course, she did not remember me. I had been little more than a child when I last served her, and who looked at staff, anyway? I might as well have been invisible, back then. It was strange to be seen, talked to, as if I was a different creature now.

"You are the liaison."

It was an odd word for it, too stylish for my role as a glorified note-taker, but I agreed. I gave my name, and held up my notebook and pencil.

She turned to the guards that stood on either side of the door to the pinnacle. I watched her draw them into her plans, gesturing with her hands, as if to physically gather them.

The tower beyond that door had not been occupied since my arrival at Crag; the rumour was that a prisoner had last been held there centuries earlier. Now it was in use again, and I would enter it momentarily. It was a thrilling thought, as if one could walk into a piece of history.

An entirely different class of conversation, Fider used to say, *lives in the remit of the diplomat. Listen, yes, but also look. The body gives much away.*

"May I call you Elize? Would you mind?"

I nodded.

The Allynx, her attention fixed on me once more, inclined her head. How graceful she was, how polite.

"You have been given instructions?"

I repeated them back to her.

"Exactly so. He is being prepared for our visit now. It should be a matter of moments." Her hand went to the folds of her dress, and retrieved an item from her pocket, which she brought to her lapel. It was in the shape of an oster in profile, with one heavy diamond eye. Its paws were raised to its chin, tucked up, and its tail nearly touched its blunt nose, turning it into a circle. It looked frightened to me, stunned into a frozen position by some horrible circumstance. It was not an item I would ever have chosen to wear myself. Why had she not opted for the famed Allynx? Was that not her symbol, her attitude?

Her hands trembled too much to affix the brooch in place. "Help me with this, if you would," she said. I reached up and took it from her fingers. I didn't comment, and neither did she, as the pin pierced the lapel, and I guided it into the hook to keep it in place.

I stepped back to a respectful distance. "There," I said. "It's secure."

"Thank you."

It was a long time since I had been so close to diamonds. The grand hall in the Mutuality had been bedecked with finery, topped with chandeliers that wept such gems. Had the Allynx been in the crowd on the night Mondegreen hung from the tightrope above us? No, I could not remember her presence on that occasion. She had only attended one time, taking afternoon tea at a party for diplomats and dignitaries—a staid affair that she had enlivened with her smile and gracious manner. But there were other cities, and they were famous for their travelling natures. How well had she already known him, before she'd captured him and delivered him to Beck's door?

"What are you thinking about?" the Allynx asked me, and I snapped my thoughts back to the present. She was looking at me with such curiosity.

"Go ahead," said one of the guards, ending the moment before I had to find an answer. The Allynx straightened her shoulders, raised her chin, and walked into the chamber that housed the one and only Mondegreen.

CHAPTER FIVE

I DID NOT look at him.

I kept my eyes on the straw-covered floor of the pinnacle, negotiating the way to the chair I had been told to claim as my own. It was in the far corner, opposite his bed; I felt his presence there, discerned his outline in shadow. The room was circular, the walls curved—of course, it was the highest point of Crag, at the very top of the staircase reserved for higher ranks, with access only from the administrative floor, where Warden Beck's own office lay. It was as bleak as any of the cells below, if a little larger. The walls were plain, and there was only one window, delineated into three apertures by two vertical bars. A curious thing: the bars made no difference. They would be easy for a man to squeeze between. Mondegreen could have thrown himself out, but only to his death, so high were we above the ground. It was a mocking reminder of that one freedom, even as it afforded a view to the north of the lake, and Stravatch, beyond. The spectacular view only served to show off the sheer drabness of the room.

I took the seat that had been placed for me, in the dark far corner, along from the window. I would barely have the light for writing. I shrank against the hard wood, and busied myself with my paper and pencil. What would I write? In the end I settled for the date and time. Then I risked a glance at the Syld, directing my gaze carefully.

She stood by the door, waiting.

Once it had been firmly shut and locked from the outside, she leaned against it, very smoothly, and crossed her legs at the ankles.

"You're still here," she said, in a tone of mild surprise. "Surely these walls pose no difficulty to you. Or are you enjoying the beauty of this austere and unusual building?"

"Did you not once tell me, Archetta, that you thought it a monstrosity made from natural material? Strange, then, to find you standing within it as if you endorse its existence."

I had expected a cracked cadence, a broken tone. Crag did that to its prisoners within hours of arrival. I'd heard it often. But Mondegreen had a strong, clear voice, with the rounded tones of the elite: cultured, and the speech so finely judged, that I suspected he had been practising it, knowing she would arrive and make some jibe. And her first name: Archetta. He knew her well.

"You're right," she said. "As ever, Marius, you are right. I wonder what the attraction could be? It's certainly not the décor. Although I think you have the best room in the place. It's bigger than the warden's room, wouldn't you say, Elize?"

My first name sounded utterly incongruent on her lips, in this room. It felt like a transgression. I kept my eyes on the floor, sitting as still as it was possible to be.

"Will you not answer me?"

I opened my mouth, shut it again. I could not play this game.

"To come all this way to be cruel to an administrator," said Mondegreen, "is beneath you."

"I'm simply establishing the rules. She is not allowed to talk, and you are not allowed to so much as look at her. And nobody is allowed to touch, isn't that right? So we will keep our distance, while we discuss this war, and how to end it. Do we all agree to abide by that?"

"Is that your real intent, Archetta?" he said.

"What a strange question."

"You want to end the war?"

"Have I not said so? Am I not to be believed?"

"Then I will play by the rules, for there's surely nothing I want more."

"Elize?" the Allynx asked me. What could I say? To speak, to assert, would be to break the very promise I had made. I was aware of her eyes on me, and perhaps I imagined his attention also glued, but I felt something, some force of personality, weighing me, waiting upon me.

I put the pencil to paper, and wrote:

I WILL

Was it bending, or breaking, the rules of this straightest of games? Dry-mouthed, I held it up to the room.

Mondegreen laughed.

It was a warm, open, free sound. I felt a smile instantly rise inside me, and I pushed it down, swallowed hard.

"Good," said the Syld. "She has written her assent. Then we'll start tomorrow. Come, Elize." She knocked on the door.

The relief at reaching the end of this first brief meeting allowed me to relax enough to risk a glance at Mondegreen. I saw the curve of his shoulder, and the line of his thigh. He sat cross-legged on the bed, which bore white linen, and a pillow that looked soft and deep. Better than my own. His shirt, too, was white, and very clean, and his long hair loose over his shoulders. This was the Mondegreen I remembered, although there were lines upon the forehead and around the eye that were marks of the passage of time. Apart from that, my first sight of him could have been yesterday. I felt a sudden, unaccountable urge to cry, but I walked past both him and the Syld with, I hope, a dignified expression. She followed behind me, and the door was locked up by guards, who then took a respectful step back.

"I'm sorry," she said. I had to steel myself to look at her, to stand my ground. My instinct as she stepped closer was to run away, find a safe place, burrow down into it and stay until these events had passed me by, forgotten about me entirely. I felt seen, used. "It was not fair, but I needed to ascertain what he would do. His response has told me many things. It has given me the advantage I need in these negotiations. Do you understand?"

"I can't claim to."

"Indeed. I promise you, I am sorry. I knew I risked you. Duty is a strange thing," she said. "I see it working upon you. Return tomorrow, and we'll start afresh on our mission."

"To end the war?" I asked.

"Of course," she said. "Of course."

CHAPTER SIX

"An interesting experience, I would have thought," said Warden Beck. "This way."

I had expected to be summoned to his office once more, but instead he sent instructions for me to meet him at the entrance to the allotments, where a side gate gave way to a heavily fenced area of relatively flat ground. Some prisoners were allowed to farm vegetables there, and the ground was divided into small square plots, meticulously kept, with strips of tough grass between them.

Beck led the way through the checkpoint, taking a sharp left turn to follow the perimeter fence. I recognised a few plants in the moonlight: runner beans, winding around canes tied in place with string, and the frothy heads of fennel. The smell of warm garlic lingered. I had seen the bright sunshine through the window of the pinnacle; it would have been pleasant to have my own patch of garden in which to enjoy it.

Beck strolled, but his legs were long. I trotted alongside him, which left me a little out of breath as I gave him an overview of that first meeting between the Syld and her catch. I tried to be both succinct and accurate. Could I find some insight for him, some facet of Mondegreen's personality, as yet unknown? I couldn't, and didn't trust myself to even try. In the end I settled for short, sharp sentences that spoke of the oster brooch, and the exchange about ending the war.

"That's what she said?" asked Beck.

"Yes, sir."

"Incredible. Perhaps she means to win him over to our side. To the idea of a greater good, even."

We reached the first corner of the garden. A wooden lean-to had been erected to hold and protect the gardening tools. It was not a sturdy structure—it looked as if it had slumped, sunk into the grass a little, as if not wanting to be noticed. Beck swerved around it, nearly walking into my path.

"Apologies," he said, then, "Did they speak of Droad?"

"No, sir." Perhaps he found that surprising.

"Tell me if they do," he said.

Droad had taken the best parts of culture from both of our sides to form the Mutuality: a place of governance that brought hope to all peace-loving people, and many in the south found it impossible to understand why the north would have targeted it. A massive explosion had wiped it utterly from the map, creating the chasm into which the galleries, theatres, markets and people had all fallen. It was a deep crack in the world from which nobody had climbed, and the ground itself there was still somehow poisoned. Nobody lived there still.

It wasn't only a question of why such a terrible act had been committed, but *how*. The technology evaded us, and when prisoners were questioned, the subject of Droad was always raised. Could we find out how they had developed such a weapon? How could we gain such capability ourselves? We lived in fear, in expectation, that they would someday use that terrible weapon again.

Beck stopped walking at the midpoint in the perimeter and inspected the nearest plot. Carrots grew there, their loose upper leaves looking healthy. He leaned over them, keeping his knees straight, and pulled up one slender, straw-like carrot. It was too early in the season; it had been interrupted in its growth. He shook off the soil and took a bite, then threw the fronded top over his shoulder. It collided with the fence, and fell to the ground.

I pictured the gardener of this patch—a prisoner with only this to care about—arriving in the morning and finding that one hole, a gap in the row, an unaccountable attack on their marshalled troops. Perhaps they would think an animal was responsible. They might not even suspect that the warden came down here, looking over their hard work as his own somehow, taking what he wanted as his right. Maybe they would hate him, if they knew.

"You didn't speak throughout," he said, once he had finished crunching.

"No, sir." I explained about the paper—the two words I had written there.

He started walking once more, and I went with him. "But he didn't look at you."

"Not as I know. I…" I had to admit it: "I'm reluctant to look at him, I—I don't want to—"

"Your job is to observe what transpires. How can you do that if you are not using your eyes, Janview? Is this assignment not suitable for you after all?"

I felt a sharp tang of fear at the thought he might take the meetings away from me. "I can observe, sir," I said. "I will do my best. I am—not used to this kind of assignment."

"Get it right. All of it."

We turned the final corner and faced the gate once more. "Oh, and Janview? Leave the notebook and pencil with the guards at the pinnacle from now on. You may record your observations as soon as you emerge, if you feel you must. Personally, I'd rather you used your memory, since you can't be trusted with paper."

We reached the main gate, and he nodded to the guard, who opened the way. His private secretary—an older man called Tarklow who shared many of his strict characteristics including immaculate posture—waited under the archway before the main courtyard.

"Urgent," Tarklow said, and handed him a message. I caught a glimpse of neat, handwritten words, then deliberately looked away. Beck swore, once, then crumpled the paper in his hand.

"Is she ready for dinner?" he asked.

"In your office, sir. You want to go ahead?"

"Of course." Beck turned to me. "Tomorrow."

I watched him stride away, the secretary a pace behind him, and saw how every guard straightened as he passed by. His power, defined by his role, borne with such rigidity of purpose, was absolute in this place. So too, then, was his responsibility for whatever happened within it. I was glad not to stand in his shoes, even if he could take whatever he wanted without retribution.

CHAPTER SEVEN

A RUNNER FOUND me over breakfast the next morning and informed me of a late start to the questioning. Instead the Syld had an intriguing errand for me, and in order to accomplish it I was handed a thing much prized in Crag: a handwritten pass from Warden Beck granting me access to all areas of the prison, without question. Word would soon get around that my status had changed. I could already see a new measure of respect in the runner's eyes as she wished me a good day.

The back stairs were used mainly by the kitchen staff to shift trays, vats and indifferent meals to the prisoners on the first twelve levels of Crag. The cylindrical stone steps started out in the kitchen, busy as ever, and I slipped through the ranks of the cooks at work, heading for the giant fireplace and the entrance to the steps beyond.

I caught the eye of one of the cooks and she told me I reminded her of her daughter, at the front, and gave me a pastry. It was, it seemed, a good day for gifts. I thanked her, pastry in hand, and took the first twelve levels of the staircase at speed. There, by the barred window before the final level, I caught my breath, then ate my treat with a view out over the lake.

The two peaks, Gryfer and Grampeg, formed the great gateway to the mountainous land of the north. They flanked the blue water, the picture of serenity, bisected by the wake from the approaching ferry to create the illusion of symmetry. Greenish ripples from the churned-up algae, disturbed by the prison ferry's propeller, fanned the surface.

The prison ferry, barely bigger than a beetle from this vantage point, chugged toward Crag. I watched it, finishing my pastry, feeling blessed with time and silence: those two great commodities, so dear to purchase in this place. I felt that just a short time in their company could restore me, give me strength to sit in that cell with Mondegreen and the Syld, and bear witness to their conversation.

Could they really bring an end to the war? Perhaps, if Mondegreen had information about the great weapon that had destroyed Droad. If we built our own version, would that bring us to a wary stalemate? I hated the idea of that kind of peace, bought with the threat of destruction, but I would take it. I did not know anyone who would not.

The ferry moved beyond my line of sight, and a thick bank of cloud swept up from behind the mountains and covered the sun. The moment of reflection was over. I sighed, turned away, and climbed the final flight of steps to the storage area.

The guard on the door checked my pass with a raised eyebrow. "You're new," he said.

"Not at all."

"Where you from?"

"Downstairs."

He looked at me blankly, and unlocked the thick metal door with a large key slung from his waist, then stepped back to let me through. Only once I was past, and I could hear him locking me in, did I realise he meant to enquire what part of the world I'd been born in. I wondered why it mattered. Maybe it didn't; maybe it was simply the question of a bored man on a long duty, looking for small talk.

I could not see why this particular room would need its own guard at all. It was a long, dusty hall, nothing more than a storage area, filled with wooden crates with the lids thrown back, as if someone had rummaged through them all and not bothered to reseal them. Long, thin windows covered with the usual bars ran the length of the north wall, letting in slanting sunlight in which motes danced; I sneezed, and scanned the sides of the crates for a clue as to what they held. Nothing was marked.

The Syld's instruction had been precise: *choose one object from one crate. Any object. Any crate. Bring it with you, when you come to the pinnacle.*

It felt like a test. Not of him, but of me.

No, it must mean that it did not matter what I brought. I chose a crate at random, one close to the door, and looked inside. I saw pieces of cracked pottery, cups with missing handles, bent forks and spoons, and more of that fine dust upon every item. Tiles and knives and pots. A rolling pin. This had been the contents of someone's kitchen once. These things had been gathered and forgotten, and everything bore marks of damage, as if the boxes had been picked up and shaken by giant hands.

The next crate contained items that were harder to identify. Scraps of material hung from metal spokes, and cubes of wood bore the remains of bright colours. Eventually it came to me. Toys. I was holding the remnants of a small drum, a doll, and building blocks.

Each crate revealed salvage from some other room in what must have been a grand house, or maybe many such homes. Destruction had been wreaked upon them all.

Eventually I found my answer when I came across the spine of a book, somehow wedged inside the nest of a drawer with iron reinforcements. All the paper within had been destroyed, the nubs of the pages singed, but I could read the title, printed in gold lettering only made brighter by whatever had befallen it:

Droad Traders & Resources Vol 588

The annual compendium of businesses was a stalwart volume on every merchant's shelf in the city. It would be of no interest to anyone else.

I was picking through the remains of Droad.

It made no sense. Why bring such vast amounts of detritus from the ruins to Crag? And then leave them here, in a storeroom, under the care of an armed guard?

How did the Syld even know of this room, these remains?

I replaced the spine in the crate, once more in the drawer that had protected it. But the drawer itself was done; it shifted and gave under the weight, the wood brittle between the iron struts. To be transported all this way only to snap now—tears came to my eyes. Ridiculous. There was no end to this loss. There was always more to be broken.

The front of the drawer had retained a curved ceramic handle. I put my hand to it, dusted it off, and colours of green and blue were revealed in a geometric pattern. I could picture it, one of a set, lined up on this grand chest of drawers, well made, gracing the office of a well-to-do trader in the city. Possibly living in one of the villas on the seaside, high above the circular fishing boats that collected nets of eels very early each morning, that were stacked on the shore by midday, with the eels taken to market to be dusted in flour and fried. The smell, drifting through the busy market with its colourful stalls. That delicate taste, slippery and salty on the tongue.

It took only the smallest amount of pressure to snap the handle from the wood. I pocketed it and took it to the pinnacle, to be given over to a new life: as an object used in the struggle to find peace.

CHAPTER EIGHT

"What shall we talk about?" said the Syld.

I had expected her to dress in plain grey, the same as yesterday—perhaps to even adorn the lapel with the same oster brooch, which had felt like a pointed statement I could not decipher—but her choice that morning underlined how little I knew her. She wore a long velvet gown, in dark blue, that was high at the neck and low to her workmanlike ankle boots, the leather well-used and scuffed at the toes.

A folding wooden chair had been brought into Mondegreen's cell for her, and placed in the centre of the room. As soon as the door was shut behind us and I had taken up position in my corner, she moved the chair forwards, only a few inches from the bed. Mondegreen was sitting with his legs crossed, his elbows resting on his knees. I was determined to watch him—to watch them both—as closely as I could. That was my remit.

"Whatever would suit your mood... The weather? The food? Your latest amour?" he asked her easily, with a slight smile.

"All thrilling subjects, of course, but I rather thought this might provide a topic." She took the object I had retrieved from the storeroom from one of her long, bell-shaped sleeves and placed it on her lap. "All the way from Droad. Or the chasm that remains, I should say. A project has been underway, ostensibly under Beck's orders, to search through the detritus for evidence."

His smile did not move, and that was how I knew it was faked, fixed in place, like a bluffer stiffly holding their cards. "Archetta," he said. "You'll be the death of us."

"I'm guessing you weren't expecting to sit so close to proof of your crimes." She threw it, a soft underhand lob, to land beside him on the bed.

He flinched, the smallest withdrawal. One twitch of the hand closest to the object, one blink of his eyes. He wanted nothing more than to move away, I was certain of it. I was beginning to be able to read him, and the thought pleased me. Then I disliked myself for feeling that way in the face of his discomfort.

"I had hoped for a different outcome," he said. "Must it be this way?"

He was afraid. Of her? Afraid of the object. I looked at it again. The handle of a drawer. It meant nothing, provoked nothing—except my own memories. It was beyond unlikely that I had managed to choose an item from a room of hundreds that would cause such a strong reaction. How could the Syld have known I would choose the exact thing needed to get under his skin? It had to be sheer chance. And yet I felt played, manipulated, in this intensely dangerous game. She had bet upon the outcome, on me, and I had come through for her. I could see it in her expression: the carefully masked delight of one who has won the round, but has many hands left to play. I was starting to read her tells, too.

"Are you anxious?" she said, suddenly.

"Always."

His smooth, immediate reply caught her by surprise. She shifted in her chair. "The legend is that you are immune to such emotions."

"If anyone would know that as a falsehood, it would be you."

"You presume I still know you well?"

"Isn't that how you caught me?"

She smiled broadly. "I do know you," she said. There were layers of intimacy in her tone I could not begin to unpick.

"But you'll make me say out loud what you know I think."

"Say it."

"Please." The word cost him something. "Please don't cause such damage that nothing can recover. I do not speak only of our own futures. There are other lives at stake."

His emphasis on the pluralities of whatever came next, the separation of their paths, was unmistakeable, and I watched the Syld absorb his meaning. There would be a time beyond this. She took it with a nod, then she reached over and took back the object, and placed it between the legs of her chair.

"Shall we talk of Droad, then?" she asked. It was precisely the topic I had been warned to listen out for. I listened intently, determined to have something useful to report back that might make sense of the role I had been given.

"Isn't that the past?"

"It was a beautiful city," she said.

"People say such things, but we both know no city is truly beautiful. They are all masses of humanity waging a daily battle to stay unburied in their own excrescence. Everyone shovels, in a city. The days are long and hard and busy, and those that can walk through its streets without taking up the work of its upkeep are truly fortunate."

"Cannot one shit in a bucket without still enjoying the view?"

He laughed, with surprise and generosity. "I've not heard that expression before," he said.

"I just invented it." She looked more than a little pleased with herself, and I liked her for her joy in her own ability to amuse. Maybe this wasn't all about provoking Mondegreen to a response. There were things they had in common, and one of those things was a delight in a sharp turn of phrase.

"This is new, this worrying about death," she observed. "It does not suit you."

"It's not *my* death that concerns me."

"That is... touching."

They both looked down, at the object under the chair.

If it was a weapon, he could have used it. In that moment, he could have snatched it up and made a bid to escape. Killed me, killed the Syld, the guards, whoever stood between him and his freedom.

It's not a weapon, I told myself. *It's a drawer handle. It's an amount of fuss about a drawer handle.* I breathed out, sharply, and the Syld's head snapped up. Her stare found me, and I read her irritation. Maybe she really had forgotten my presence in the room. Then that smooth, gracious expression returned, and she moved her gaze, slowly and deliberately, from me to Mondegreen.

He was not looking at me. He was too good a player to lose a game so easily, at the first hint of distraction. His eyes were closed, his breathing regular. He looked peaceful.

"Talk of Droad," she commanded, and he did.

WHAT STRUCK ME later, while I waited in the garden for Warden Beck's arrival, was how personal Mondegreen's words had felt. I don't mean that they sounded emotional, or heartfelt. He talked without hesitation of the city as he remembered it, as if passing time in the past, as people do. But as he spoke, a feeling grew upon me. I began to think he was not speaking for the Syld's benefit, or because of her instruction. A creeping warmth overtook me with each street and square he conjured, and every avenue he defined. His Droad was my own.

He drew it for me. I can't explain it any more than that. He drew it with precise, loving lines, and breathed it into life. The destruction of Droad had been a terrible loss, not only in terms of the people who had died and I had mourned, but for the curves of the red walls and the blue domes, the gaudy stalls of the markets, the saplings on the avenues and the carts selling fruit on the cobbled streets. The smell of Droadcake along Bakery Way, and the fresh tang of the seafront, rich traders and poor thieves and poor traders and rich thieves, mingling, disguised as each other. And games! Children playing chalk games, and the old emerging from their tall terraces to attend the numerous Hatted events, with the diversions to gamble upon, jugglers and fire-eaters and mechanical races, metal jockeys riding through the gardens on their ponies. The Mutuality's many diversions, the heart of the city, where both sides met and held good faith with each other, and we had all thought peace was possible where joy thrived.

Yes, it was a loss, and Mondegreen understood that, and mourned it.

And yet he had chosen the other side.

Beck arrived and we walked the same circuit as yesterday. He chose a different patch to plunder, pulling up a radish, which he nibbled upon, then threw over the fence. There was a weed growing in the next patch along: a dandelion. It was tough, tall, a stray between the feathery fronds of fennel plants. It had been there long enough to bloom, and had become a clock of seeds, waiting for the right moment to spread, given a helpful gust of wind, to plant itself elsewhere and begin again.

I recounted the conversation as we walked. It sounded different to my ears, but I knew I couldn't communicate where the difference lay. It hurt to hear my own voice ruin the way he had flowed through memories like water.

"Did they talk of how Droad was destroyed?"

"No, sir."

"Not a mention?"

"Never. But she bid me bring in an object that had survived the attack. I collected it from the twelfth floor. A handle, to an old drawer. It... unbalanced him."

"Unbalanced him? How?"

"He watched it carefully." A pang of guilt came to me, as if I had betrayed a confidence, but I pushed it down.

"Where is this item now?" said Beck.

"The Syld returned it to my keeping. I'm meant to return it to the storeroom tomorrow."

"Bring it to me," he said, and I could picture him puzzling

over it, turning it between his long fingers, much as he had dusted off the vegetables before consuming them.

"Are they... flirtatious?" he asked.

We reached the back shed, where the tools of the day were stacked. "They know each other well," I said. "I wouldn't term it as attraction."

"Wouldn't you?"

"There is history between them."

"History may present as shared emotion when there is nothing but experience," mused Beck. "You are right. It may not be current feeling. I like your ability to avoid jumping to obvious conclusions, Janview. Keep it up." He stopped walking, and looked out to the rocks beyond the fence, where the climb began to the mountains that dominated the north. How dark it was, in those jagged corners. "How exhausting this will be. Let's hope the Syld does not intend to play the long game here."

"Sir?"

He dismissed me, with final orders to deliver the item to his secretary, who would know what to do with it.

That would make one of us, I thought.

By the time the job was done I had missed dinner, and gambling seemed far less enticing on an empty stomach. I retreated to the barracks, and slept deeply, surprisingly, until Tommo shook me awake in the early hours with news that the enemy's attack on Stravatch had started.

CHAPTER NINE

ON THE BATTLEMENT, next to the line of the cannons, we stood together: Imberley, Tommo and I. We were high enough for the air to be thin and hard in the lungs.

"Where's Pappas?" said Imberley.

"Lost a bet for a shift in the eight," said Tommo. Eight was one of the closed units; he wouldn't be out for a while.

"Shame to miss this," Imberley mused, and I knew exactly what she meant. It was a fearsome sight, but I was glad to witness it myself rather than hear about it second-hand. Would description have done it justice? Maybe, from the mouth of Mondegreen. Other than that, I don't think I would have believed it.

Stravatch was on fire.

It was a dawn, an awful rising of first light, but not a clean glow: dirty oranges and reds from black columns of smoke so thick their smell reached us. It obliterated the town from view. All that was visible was the harbour, and the white façade of the old fish hall, a prominent building before the stone quay.

"They've used the weapon again," Imberley said.

"No," I said. "Look. Things still stand."

The smoke had its own rhythm, and would thin sometimes, just enough to reveal the town underneath. There were many fires, and no doubt many losses, but it could still be called Stravatch. This was the work of the heavy guns, weapons we knew and possessed ourselves. I did not want to find that comforting, but there was no denying it was preferable to the alternative. I had no idea why I would rather die from the familiar, but it was undoubtedly so.

"There," said Tommo, pointing. He stood closer to the edge of the parapet than I would have dared myself. How straight and fearless he looked there, overseeing the devastation. "The ferry."

Yes, I could make it out. It was sailing without lights, a shadow on the water, not far out of the town. We watched it approach at an inchingly slow speed, but it was progressing. Escaping. My teeth clenched, my hands shaking in the cold, I watched it.

"They've spotted it," murmured Imberley, beside me. Lights were gathering in Stravatch harbour. The fish hall had a lick of orange to its roof. It wouldn't stand long.

Would they fire upon the ferry?

It was defenceless.

Every time I drew a line under the behaviour of those we fought—told myself: *no further than this or I will become nothing but hate*—they crossed it.

"Three wraps it is sunk," breathed Imberley.

It grew closer. What had looked, at distance, to be a smooth movement revealed itself to be a surging crawl, and a list— not much, but enough to call it a bad bet. Still, I said, "It will make it."

"You taking the odds, then?"

The side of the ferry dipped lower. The lights in the harbour had intensified. They were gathering. Surely they had seen the boat. It could be only a matter of minutes until they fired upon it.

"Last chance," said Imberley.

I glanced at Tommo, the tense lines of his shoulders and the straight cut of his hair across the back of his neck. He was very beautiful to me. I said, "You're on."

Lower sunk the side of the ship. Slow was its progress.

Lower.

The lights in Stravatch harbour were strong. A beam of fat white light cast out over the water, cutting along the lake. Searching.

Lower.

But I could breathe again, I could let the cold burn my lungs, for the ferry was at the jetty, the shouts of those onboard audible, rising up to us. Someone fell from the side of the ferry into the water, and for a heartbeat I thought they would be crushed between boat and jetty, but they scrambled up and a rope was thrown to them, and looped around one of the iron moorings. People jumped to safety, then began to help others across the divide of the water. Children were lifted out, carried up towards the gates of Crag.

Tommo stepped back from the edge and pushed past us, taking the steep stone steps at speed. The people would need blankets, hot drinks, maybe food. Beds. There would be much to organise.

"I owe you three wraps," said Imberley, glumly, and I nodded. Yes, she owed me, and there would be time for her to pay up before the enemy made it to Crag. As we descended and began the business of helping those who had lost everything, that was what I thought about: the wraps I would get, and what I could bet them on next. It was by far the safest space in which to keep my mind.

CHAPTER TEN

Who was the enemy?

I could not picture the prisoners of Crag as a threat to me. They were unfortunates with broken wills, miserable but not vindictive. I think if they had been determined to look upon me with hate I could have reciprocated, but in some cases I had found the opposite to be true. A few had thanked me for the sense of fairness I brought to their captivity, without rancour, without smugness.

Not long into my second year at Crag I was allocated washblock duty, handing out soap and towels from a long bench as they filed past, waiting their turn for a private cubicle. Beck insisted on dignity for all. An older woman with a scarred face and slumped shoulders passed by with her eyes fixed on mine. She wore the rank tabs of a

Commander, but all trace of leadership had left her. She said, "Bless your rules." I had wondered: did she mean to thank me personally, or was she grateful for a system that did not demand her nakedness, her diminishment? I thought for a long time that she should have thanked Beck. Wasn't he the heart of morality that pumped inside these walls? If he caved, demanded monstrosities of us, wouldn't we all follow suit?

The box that had held the man: was this not the first loss of that famed dignity?

As we helped escapees of Stravatch make their way from the ferry, I found my mind returning to that commander at the washblock. Those deep scars on her face, and that humble blessing. The enemy for so many of us was the war itself, and those who took delight in it as an excuse to undermine what was good about humanity.

Of course, all is not so simple; sometimes rules must be bent in the face of suffering. The difficulty lies in knowing which ones.

"No access," said the guard on duty, when we tried to lead the first arrivals through to the warmth of the hall.

I stared at her: a young woman, around my age, her face clean and untouched and shuttered against whatever I would say. It was unbelievable that she would watch those in need freeze without standing aside. And yet she was on duty, and she had been given orders. I didn't know her.

Tommo came up behind me, carrying a toddler who shivered in his arms, with men and women behind him. He looked every inch a hero. He nodded to the guard; he knew her.

"Starke," he said.

"I'm under orders," she said, in a low voice, soft, and I understood then that they knew each other well. "Were you told to be down here? I didn't see your name on the roster."

"We saw the attack."

"So?"

He moved quickly, as if he would simply walk through her, and she was ready for him, braced against the gate. "Don't be an idiot," she said, contemptuous. He was bigger, but she knew he would not test her. He stopped, inches from her, the child between them, who looked from one face to the other with a small frown.

I thought about it. I thought of striking her, leading them all to the warmth of the great fire in the long room, and I would become a hero and a villain at the same time.

It was not to be. One of the sergeants emerged and said to Starke, "It's secure." Starke moved to one side, and did not look at Tommo as he passed. We all followed after him.

Inside, the hall was being transformed; many hands were at work, setting up cots and bringing down blankets. I could smell soup and fruit bread, and the fire had been stacked with wood to make a flame brighter than I'd ever seen in that giant hearth. We came together, caring for those in need, and I was ashamed that I had ever doubted my compatriots, or imagined it necessary to take matters into my own hands.

There was much to do.

I caught sight of Warden Beck, sleeves rolled, serving tea, and even saw Tarklow, that dour figure, rocking a baby while its mother ate. Just as I thought every available person had come to help, I realised: of the Allynx Syld, there was no sign.

The ferry was not the only boat to make it across the lake that night. Others arrived in smaller craft, exhausted and in trauma—some unable yet to speak—and we found a place in the hall for them all, caught in the rhythm of plying them from their vessels and leading them into the warmth. For a while I lost myself in this pattern, able to push away all thoughts of the misery over the water, until I looked up and realised it was approaching mid-morning, and the sun had climbed high enough to escape the pall of smoke that hid Stravatch from view. Who knew what crimes were being committed under that cover? But the lake was clear and serene once more, and there was only one more small fishing boat out on the water, drifting up to the beach.

I trotted down to the edge of the shingle, feeling the muscles of my legs and shoulders twinge from a night of such exertion, but I bore their complaints and waded in to pull the prow towards the shore. A man lay inside, on his back in bilge water, and I shouted to him until he roused himself, watching with relief as he leapt from the boat and managed to help me pull the boat to dry ground.

When the boat was secure, the man turned to me, grasped my hand. I felt a shock of recognition as powerful as any weapon. Fider.

He had shrunk into himself, the skin of his face pouched, grizzled with stubble, and such fear and pain hanging on him, like a cloak. But without a doubt, even with the weight of our years apart upon him, and all the terror of the night just passed, I knew him. How could I ever forget him? My dead tutor, returned to life: Fider.

CHAPTER ELEVEN

HOW TO BELIEVE it? No time for questions; he was so cold, shivering, on the last dregs of his energy. He half-collapsed against me and I managed to get him up the beach, to the gate. I felt him flinch as we passed under the portcullis.

Starke was still on duty; she had watched the doors to the hall all night. She gave me a weary nod, and asked, "Any more?"

"The last," I said, and at that moment Fider started, and pulled back from me, and I thought he had heard my voice, and had not until that moment known me. I steered him through the rows of cots to the back of the hall, my favoured place now repurposed, and found him an empty cot. He slumped into it, his head in his hands.

"Rest," I said. "A long night."

He didn't reply.

Well, it had been a stupid thing to say. This was a man with whom I had discussed so many subjects, ranging through time and space, all fearlessly tackled in talks that had pushed into hours in order to put me right comprehensively, but sure: *a long night.*

I wanted him to look up and see me. I wanted to be certain that he knew me, and was glad, and grateful of my continued existence when he had every reason to think me dead. That was what I had thought of him.

"I…" I began, and he made a sound, somewhere between a sigh and groan, that came from deep inside him.

"You don't know me," he said.

It was him. His voice.

"But I—"

"You don't know me, and if anyone asks I will be clear that I don't know you." He leaned down and started to untie his boots, and I watched him for a while: the process of loosening his laces with his shaking, dirty fingers.

He had made me feel ridiculous twice in as many minutes. In that respect, at least, he had not changed.

"Janview!"

Across the busy hall, Captain Shird awaited me. It would be an offence to refuse to answer a summons. I straightened up and adjusted my collar, then tried to walk smartly to her side. My legs were weak; they would barely take my weight. Nothing was as it had been, only minutes before.

"I seem to be turning into your messenger," she said, but I thought I saw a gleam of sympathy in her hooded eyes. "You've got an hour. Get some sleep. Then fetch something from the twelfth, and report for special duty."

"Something, sir?"

"I'm told you'll understand. That'll make one of us."

Something. What thing? Anything.

She dismissed me, and I fled the hall to find my own private bunk, just for an hour, where I could sink into escape from fire, and flame, and a past that had caught up with me yet again, then refused to admit that it knew me at all.

CHAPTER TWELVE

AND SLEEP, SLEEP had the same quality as answers: a small amount was worse than none. I fell into dreamlessness, then was awakened with a jolt by the duty sergeant. I felt I had travelled far and moved nowhere at all.

I had once longed to know if anyone from my old life had escaped Droad, and over time had come to accept that nobody remained. Only a freakish set of circumstances had led to my own survival, after all. Finding out Fider was still alive brought me great pleasure, but I awoke filled with questions. Why had he come to Stravatch? Had he been there since Droad's destruction? Did he not care to know what had happened to me? Why did my old tutor refuse to know me, and how did he manage to flee Droad when so very few had? It was a feat worthy of Mondegreen himself.

Speaking of the great man, I took myself to the usual session with the Syld, and could not help but stare at him: the long, proud lines of his neck and nose, and the lank mess of his hair where it fell over his forehead. Perhaps he could feel my eyes upon him. He cleared his throat, a little.

The Syld did not speak.

She stood by the one window split into three, close to my chair, looking out at the view—or, rather, at the lack of it. All was smoke, thick smoke. I could smell it, taste it.

The latest object from the twelfth floor lay on the bed.

I had chosen it from the crate nearest the door, refusing to get sucked into the business of caring about this nonsensical task. Whatever came to hand would do, and what found its way into my palm was a bolt, from a door perhaps, or a chest. A good size, sheared through. Rusted. An object both plain and eloquent, speaking of the sheer force of the blast that had destroyed Droad. When I had given it to the Syld, outside the door of the cell, she had given a small, satisfied smile. Had she predicted my choice yet again? Was I so transparent to her?

"Things are alight," Mondegreen remarked, casually, as if to nobody at all.

"Yes." The Syld returned to her own chair, and arranged herself on the hard seat. "The town burns."

"Don't we all?"

"All?"

"The three of us," he said, and I felt colour flood to my

face, it could not be controlled; he had mentioned me. Drawn attention to me. It was as if he had looked me in the eye and held out his hand.

"The Allynx, the Oster, and the Misheard Word," the Syld said.

"Just so."

Had I understood her correctly? I had heard Mondegreen called The Misheard Word on occasion, but I was no oster. I thought of the brooch she had worn to their first meeting, in the shape of one of those quick, thick-pelted river creatures, sly of nature, good at squeezing into fishermen's baskets and stealing eels. Who was the oster in their group? Why did I feel ridiculous, as if suddenly excluded?

"Once I heard a man say there were no such things as mistakes."

"No doubt you put him straight, Archetta."

"He won't make that error again, it's true. But who would want to repeat their errors when there are so many fun fresh ones to find?"

Mondegreen's attention moved pointedly to the bolt. He did not touch it. "Is that so?"

"Am I boring you?"

"If you are, no doubt you have your reasons, and good entertainment is hard to come by just now."

"Then you'll forgive me," she said, putting one hand to her chest.

"Done—in exchange for a story."

"You wish me to speak of myself?"

"Only a bad storyteller thinks all stories must be about themselves, but yes, why not? I'm starved of narrative, Archetta. Humour me."

She dropped her hands, smoothed her dress over her thighs, pressed her lips together, and began. It was another thing she shared with Mondegreen: the act of telling a story so well that one became stuck, suspended within it. I listened in awe, in reverie, as she began:

I was a poor child from poor parentage, and when they died together from a sudden fever, on the coldest of cold nights, they left me with even less. The townsfolk of Avock, my place of birth, stripped the house before they were even in the ground, and looked through me, around me, anywhere but at me. I was expected to die too, but I was ornery, I would never listen to what was expected of me. I walked away, northwards, high into the mountains, and ate the tough grasses, drank the icy streams.

Does this sound romantic? It was the hardest of lives and I don't recommend it. But it was purifying, to live without language, without care. I realised humanity is a varnish, a thin sheen we apply. How quickly I had been made invisible, when those around me decided I was irrelevant. You strive to play this trick, Marius—the gift of the vanished—and I have always been the opposite: I want to be seen. The greatest safety net is the one in the brightest colours, woven from the thickest strands.

But I get ahead of myself.

I moved ever northwards, towards the heart of the mountains, where the peaks and sky meld and merge, and there is a solid wall of ice where the world ends. I did not get that far, of course; nobody ever had and lived, and I would not dream of claiming to have broken that last great barrier. But I grew close, and food became scarce, and the water too cold to drink. My few clothes were falling apart and I fully expected to freeze to death. I did not care much. But something in me pushed onwards, forwards. I could not sit down and wait for death to come to me. How do you do it now, Marius? Does it not drive you insane?

No, I went searching for death. I needed to seek it out, to stand in its presence, like an equal. How ridiculous. Still, it's the silliest thing that becomes the reason to continue.

You know the story, but if you need my voice to keep you going, I will give it to you. The cave. I came across the cave, the smallest of openings in a rock face over which moss grew. I ate a little of the moss, found it sustaining, and crawled inside to find a space that stretched back and back, and opened into a warm and sheltered abode, with beams of light falling through the rough rocks that formed a roof, interspersed with stalactites as sharp as knives. The warmth sent me into a stupor; I had not realised my own exhaustion. I fell down. I slept. I slept for so long, so deeply, in strange dreams of the places I had left behind.

When I awoke, I was in the presence of an Allynx.

A creature like a cat, but ten times the size. A legend. A tale told to scare children. White, curved teeth and a tongue so rough that its lick could have broken my skin. Great paws, capable of clinging to any surface, with dagger-sharp claws. And wonderful whiskers! Everything a small cat possesses, including charm, and playful moods, and moods in which it could bite your head off without guilt or regret. But it was a curious, and oddly caring beast. I don't think it had seen a human before. It took me in as an oddity. It was intelligent, and I think it recognised that quality in me. It curled up around me, and kept me warm, and when we both awoke it offered me food from its own supply of hunted goat.

Time passed. We came to an understanding. I learned its language, and it attempted to master mine. It was a poet, finding rhythm and cadence in its purring words. We lived together for a time I cannot measure, through summers and winters, and I was as close to it as it is possible to be to another creature, any creature. Then, one day, I woke and it was dead beside me, light and empty and free of this world.

I cut off its beautiful fur and wrapped myself in that final gift. I wished its corpse goodbye and set off, back across the mountains. It kept me warm through weeks of walking, and when I arrived back in Avock, that small town that had left me to die, I showed them my pelt and told them my story. It captivated the very folk who had wanted me to disappear. They paid to see it, to stroke it, to ask me their questions. I signed up with a travelling troupe and found I had learned to humour the worst of humanity, and appreciate the best of it. For instance, freshly baked bread, Marius: is it not magnificent in this establishment? The cooks really are a marvel. I say such skill represents the greatest of gifts.

"You only say that because you've never had to make your living producing hundreds of loaves a day."

"Even so, I don't think I'd tire of the smell, or the taste."

"Anything can become tiresome," observed Mondegreen. "I once disguised myself as a baker, to escape a tricky situation. Even the best bread in this land really can wear thin." He shook his head, as if she had tired him. "There are many kinds of disguise, Archetta. You may wear many layers of finery, and tell others that they witness wealth and power, or you may go naked and let others clothe you in their imagination."

"Either way, the wind blows, Marius. The wind will always blow. I think I'll keep my fur wrapped tight about me."

"You do that. It would suit no-one as well as you."

CHAPTER THIRTEEN

"A BOLT?" SAID Beck.

"A good sized one, sir. From a door or a chest, would be my guess."

"You think that relevant?"

"Respectfully, I have no idea what is relevant."

"Yes, deciding that would certainly be above your pay grade. Go on."

I related to him the story the Syld had told; he would have known it well, anyway. Everyone did. But he let me tell it in its entirety, and did not interrupt. We strolled the perimeter of the allotments, as usual. His pace was a little slower, maybe. I wondered if he wanted to take his time, to use this meeting as a respite from the challenges he faced, the worries he carried. Stravatch had been taken. Was Crag their next target?

"And thus she was transformed into an allynx herself," he said, when I'd finished. He hesitated over a small patch of flowers by the fenceline, yellow and lilac, quite gaudy. They would not have been planted by an inmate. I imagined seeds had blown through the fence, and found this swatch of untended ground—an unexpected gift to us all. Beck crouched, picked one, and sniffed it. "The less well-known tale is how she came by the title of Syld. A high rank for one from such a lowly beginning, working in the arts. Do you know that tale?"

I shook my head.

"The word is that she did a great service to a very high-ranking official." He smacked his lips together, then coughed. Then the enjoyment of the anecdote seemed to leach out of him; he looked at me, and he did not elaborate. Instead he said, "You know the traditional duty of the Sylds?"

"Gatekeepers of Peace," I said. "Holders of borders." I had served them, now and again, at the Mutuality. They were usually aged figures of the north, given to long speeches. I had assumed the Syld had been given the title as she was the only one to reach the mountains that marked the end of the world. It seemed a fitting honour, to me. I preferred that version to Beck's.

"Perhaps she brought inner peace," he mused, and I did not smile. He handed me the flower, then said, "They waste time in reminiscing, and the enemy fortify at Stravatch. We are overrun, stretched to our limits. I suspect the enemy will come fast, with urgency, if they decide Mondegreen is worth the risk. There will be much loss of life. I tell you this only so you can appreciate the question it raises—what power does he hold over them, that they would fight so hard to take him back?"

Could some answer lie in the memories the Syld and Mondegreen traded every day? Memories brought to life? I did not speak of my theory. I kept quiet, and let Beck muse until we reached the gate. Tarklow waited for him with impeccable bearing, watchful eyes, and an ever-growing list of problems, no doubt. He glanced at me swiftly, then looked away. I thought I saw a flash of speculation, of calculation in his eyes, as if I was an interesting curio with a meaning to be squirrelled out.

As I left the allotments I sniffed the flower, still in my hand, and found it smelled of nothing at all. I crumpled it, and let it fall to the hard ground.

CHAPTER FOURTEEN

OVER THE DAYS that followed I brought many items to the cell: twisted piles of glass, melted from ferocious heat, and clumps of coins, fused together. A tortoiseshell hairclip that looked untouched, brand new, and part of the head of an old stone statue, its nose and ears knocked clean off. Neither Mondegreen nor the Allynx talked about any of these items. She would place the item beside him, on his bed, each morning as we entered the room. It would sit there throughout. They fenced with words, exchanging thoughts, ideas, observations. I was never addressed, never looked at, not by either of them. I was not there. I became adept at remembering their conversations, and I found myself looking forward to the time I spent in their company, so different from the duty of care I owed to the prisoners of Crag. Even so, I felt a growing discomfort that I could not explain nor understand. What did I want? Why was it becoming more difficult to sit in silence?

It was not that I wanted to say something in particular. I knew little about the subjects they discussed. It was only that I wanted to have the right to speak, and to find the correct words on my tongue to make them turn their heads, and re-evaluate me, and maybe think I belonged in that room as an equal.

Ridiculous.

I pushed the urge down deep, and listened all the harder, trying to memorise certain phrases to relate to Beck rather than retell it with my perfunctory blandness. The nature of the conversation changed. They took to telling old tales, folk tales, some of which I remembered from my own childhood, and some from dusty books, or told to me by Fider. They took delight in them as if they'd never heard them before, and were pooling them as a collection of new and precious knowledge to be cherished.

They told stories of the north:

There was once a pale child who discovered she could breathe life into the clay made by her people, and she created a doll that was good, and kind, and would do no harm. She let it loose into her village, certain that it would be a blessing to all who came across it, so sweet was its nature. She wanted all to have a share of such innocence.

At first the villagers loved it, and treated it like a superior, fetching and carrying for it, giving it tasty bits to eat and the best stories to listen to. Then they realised that the doll did not mind if it was given the worst bits of the meal, the gristle and the peelings, and it never complained if the stories had unhappy endings. And so their behaviour worsened, and soon they were commanding the doll to do the dirty tasks they did not care for, and barely feeding it scraps, and whispering to it of their worst deeds, over and over, under the cover of a terrible darkness that had descended upon all their souls.

Then, one morning after the longest of nights, the doll—

They told stories of the south:

The greatest musician from the pastures and vineyards of Droad was nothing more than a shepherd. He had carved his own picoldo, the smallest of all the flutes, from a broken branch, while watching over his flock, and he had taught himself to play only for their benefit. Every day he played new songs for them, and he learned that when he played well, without artifice or expectation, the sheep gathered around him, and nuzzled him, and kept him warm with their wool.

One day, a passing Mutuality contingent on an important mission suffered a broken wheel, and they stopped, and got out of the listing carriage, and looked around for help. The endless plains stretched out around them. They shivered, and shouted, and then they listened for a reply. What they heard stunned them all. It was the most perfect tune, and it called to them. They followed it, across the plains, for many miles, until they reached the shepherd. They pushed the sheep aside, and huddled close to him. They said: Come with us, and play your music in our beautiful rooms. You will have the kind of rich life that such an artist deserves.

The shepherd told them he could not possibly leave his sheep, and the Mutuality contingent replied: Oh, that is easy to solve! They took out their pistols and shot every last sheep dead.

The shepherd looked at their corpses, and at the contingent. He put his lips to the picoldo and—

They told stories of the cities:

A thousand builders worked for a thousand weeks on the magnificent pillar of justice in Frietown, majestic city of the deserts, and it grew taller and taller, up to the clouds, until nobody thought it could continue to stand. But three architects of great skill were tasked by the cityfolk to keep it upright. More than that—they were given the task of helping it to pierce the clouds, and find heaven beyond. And so they set about their mission.

The three architects decided upon a plan, and sent word up the tower, to the thousand builders, detailing how to extend the length even further. Then they watched from the ground, anticipating growth. But the clouds obscured their vision, and even on clear days it was impossible to tell how much progress was being made.

So the architects climbed the tower.

One of the architects was very young, and she sprang from step to step, showing no signs of slowing down.

One of the architects was middle-aged, and he took his time, but he made progress.

The third architect was older, and he had sustained an injury to his leg, fighting in the first wars, long since ended. He could not climb far. He sat on one of the steps, and rested, and while he did so, the youngest architect reached the top, and found the builders also at rest. Fed up of living away from the comforts and securities of Frietown at ground level, they had stopped working altogether.

Give us a reason to keep going, said the builders.

And the youngest architect, removed from both patience and wisdom, said—

What stories they told!

They reminded me that this could have been a country of strange unity, sharing a love of the tales from all its corners. But that would have been a different world from the one I knew.

Then, one day, Mondegreen told a story that included me.

We both came from performative lives, Archetta, and we know the way to make a crowd see the spectacle. I have lived my life shrouded in the fine smoke of illusion, with my back to the hard wall of reality. Acts of true disappearance take... commitment.

I started my training with knife throwing. Knife catching. I still bear the scars on my fingers. Then on to the high wire. Balance. The trapeze. Sleight of hand, too. A light switched on inside me, a glow for everything I could do that others could not. It was the greatest gift to be appreciated for such skills.

But wonder never lasts forever.

I could feel it leave the crowd, drain away, and the applause would turn thin and hard. Whenever the people began to lose their taste for such tricks, I knew it was time to move on, and it's possible to see my career, my life, as an act of eternal departures, one after another. At some point I will reach a place from which I cannot find an exit when the enchantment of my reputation fails, and then I will know it is time to change profession for good. Until then, I remain—what? Let's say I am an entertainer. I prefer not to make a delineation between life before and after the outbreak of this particular war, for I believe my role remains unchanged. Some are amused when I perform, and some are moved to disdain, or to hatred. I have no control over that, although...

I've played many places. The less I liked a crowd, the more I charged to make an appearance, and it amazed me when exorbitant fees were met. I was once commissioned to play a ball at a great gathering of the high and mighty, the rich and powerful. The doors were closed to nearly all of lesser status. I say all—I do not want to fall into the trap of wealth where it's easy to pretend blindness to need, so let me state here and now that I saw them: the servers, the waiters, the cleaners. The workers, creating their own illusions that mollified those with money. I wonder if there can be a place in existence that does not share this inequality?

I strung a wire between upper balconies, and stood central, looking down upon them all. I saw a rarity, too. A youth, obviously of lower status, moving in the crowds, trying their hardest to remain unseen. I saw myself in them. I recognised that desire to be present, to be in the room where the important decisions are made. To be more than my birthright allowed. I wondered what would happen—if they would be caught and punished, and have their audacity beaten out of them.

I finished my act with the usual trick, nothing special—the removal of the coins. But this time I slipped them all to the youth. Not enough to be missed, but maybe a help to one who had little. If only power could be so easily distributed. I still think of it as my finest moment.

"You singled out someone who didn't ask for your help," said the Syld. "You knew nothing about their situation beyond what you chose to see."

"Isn't that always the way?"

"It is possible to wait to be asked for your input."

"My help wouldn't be any more deserved for being requested, would it? And I gave that child very little."

"Yes, only the illusion of help."

"The money was real!" he said, with a trace of indignance.

"But the power was not. And nor was your attention. You moved on. It's possible the child did not."

"I've always admired you, Archetta," he said. He put his hands over his face.

I wanted to go to him. I wanted to touch his shoulder, and tell him I was the youth, and the money had changed my life, given me hope, and education. And I had felt seen for the very first time. Even if he had not seen me well.

I wanted to say: *I was not a symbol of the poor, the downtrodden. I was not a victim then, nor am I now.*

I stayed in my seat.

He sighed, and took his hands down, and I could see he had not been crying, nor in the grip of any great emotion. Or perhaps he hid it very well indeed.

I TOLD BECK of the stories.

I did not tell him where they touched my own life, and I did not tell him what Mondegreen had revealed: that for all his words of praise for Droad, for all his skill at summoning the streets and gardens of that beautiful city, he had despised the rich and powerful everywhere, and may have wished them ill. Would he have destroyed it all simply to bring down the Mutuality?

How much must one hate a thing in order to destroy everything that surrounds it?

CHAPTER FIFTEEN

THE WEATHER IMPROVED as the season moved into summer, and we soldiers ate in the courtyard, under the face of the clock, while the survivors of Stravatch occupied the hall, under a watchful guard of their own.

In the main body of Crag, deep in the rock walls, the prisoners were unsettled. Some spark of life had returned.

They could not have known of the fall of Stravatch. The changes to their routines were minor. They exercised in the indoor arena, usually reserved only for team sports, which meant less time outside. And there were fewer guard changes, too, as we pulled longer shifts to compensate. But even the smallest changes may seem amplified to those who live by unbending detail, and I was often asked for news that I could not give.

Their agitation affected us. We muttered dark thoughts over our games of dice, to do with the possibility of spies, smuggled in as survivors, using the tragedy of the town to penetrate our defences. But time passed without incident, and the days grew longer, and both Tommo and Imberley reported back from their regular shifts in the hall. They spoke of finding only decent people among those who had fled. Some remained morose, catatonic, lying on their cots, barely eating and drinking. Some cried out, and were fearful. But others were calm, and keen to help. They requested work duty, or a way to aid others. I wondered if Fider was one of the silent ones, or a talker. I could not picture him as either.

We also muttered about supplies.

Crag had a water source, a well, deep in its heart; we began a programme of lowered usage for washing purposes, but drinking water was not a concern. The sealed food, too, would last a year or more, but fresh fruit and vegetables would soon start to run out without supplies from Stravatch. Beck was a man of planning. He took no chances. Extra ground was turned over for agricultural purposes, fencing extended, and the survivors were vetted, then assigned patches. It was fortunate the attack had come in warm weather, perhaps. Seeds were planted, seedlings grown. All stayed mild and the venture was successful. Some of the soldiers also volunteered for a patch—I was among them—and we were given slots, day and night, for the duty. What a uniquely fractured time it was.

One could look up from weeding and see prisoner, refugee, and guard, side by side, hard at work together.

Fider was given a patch not far from my own, at the very back of the extended fenceline, having been vetted and deemed to be a minimal risk. I nodded at him whenever one of us arrived or left, but he did not respond to the gesture. I thought I had missed him before, but to be in his presence brought an awful longing to me with a freshness, as if Droad had been ruined only days before. He was my past, my childhood, the best part of me. The before: so much richer than the after. I began to hate the thing I had become, sworn to a revenge I had no idea how to enact. My time as a guard was nearing an end, one way or another, and I still was no closer to finding someone to blame.

The prisoners who worked the ground took back news to the others, of course. It bubbled through the rocks of Crag, like water rising from a spring.

With many more people in the allotments at all times, the venue of my regular meetings with Beck was changed to a new location: the gallery. It was in the darkest part of Crag, pressed against the sheer wall of the mountain where the most disruptive prisoners were kept. Above their solitary confinement, in one long passage that ran the length of the prison, were the polished wooden floors and walls of the gallery, where paintings hung depicting Crag's history. We paced it together, Beck and I, in the dim orange light of oil lamps that left a greasy sheen in the air, and I spoke of what happened in the pinnacle. He took it all in with great care, and offered me nothing in return. Which was, of course, as it should be.

But there was a time, unique, when he stopped before a pen-and-ink illustration of Stravatch, drawn to look across the lake to Crag. It was a distorted, impossible view, with Crag extending far up into the sky, casting a giant shadow over the lake, breaking up into shards upon the water.

Beck commented on the warping of the perspective, and the crosshatch of thick black lines used to accentuate the pinnacle. "How they fear it," he said, meaning our enemy, I suppose. "And yet it has never been used in the way they imagine, until now."

"As a prison?"

"As a goad. *Throw yourself from the window; that's the only way to end your suffering.* That is what they think of us—of how inhuman we must be. But the pinnacle has only ever been one thing before the arrival of our illustrious guest. A room for the scribe to keep ledgers. Incomings, outgoings. That's why the window is barely barred. To afford light for writing. But then, Crag never was meant to be a prison at all. It was a military school, back when I first trained. They say Crag has never fallen. They are right. That is because nobody has ever attempted to make it fall. And now my advisors say we should use the stories that have arisen. It sends the right message to the enemy, and that is all that counts."

He told me this with a soft smile on his lips, and a slight shrug, as if this was all out of his control. I could not bear the thought of it. Such corruption of an innocuous place, until it had become the very worst tale told of it. "Can we not let the prisoners know all this?"

"What does it matter now, Janview?" he said. "It is their prison. They own it. Let them change it with their words, their beliefs, as they so wish." How quickly he washed his hands of his own responsibility, but I could see it pained him to do so.

A suspicion came to me. "May I ask—who suggested Mondegreen should be kept there, sir?"

"He is the Syld's captive. I have not obstructed her." Beck reached out as if to touch the picture, then pulled back his hand. "I found this in a market stall in Droad," he said. "Incongruous for this wall, perhaps, with its oils and heavy frames. But I feel it belongs here. My mark upon this gallery, too. The modern age." He started to walk once more, and murmured, "Keep going, keep going." I did not know whether he talked to me, or to himself.

WHY DID THE Syld hate him so much as to choose the pinnacle as a demonstration to all of his suffering? Was it because of Droad? Was he truly to blame? I turned it over and over in my mind. I began to choose items from the twelfth floor with more care, deliberating over them, looking for things that reminded me of the city I loved. Mondegreen's words played a part in this choosing, his memories bleeding into my own.

I chose fragments of blasted vases where the circular patterns had burned into the china.

I chose a rock into which a belt buckle had sunk, showing the insignia of the uniform worn by the city's municipal workers.

I chose an ornate twisted metal fixture that I would have sworn once held up one of the chandeliers in the Mutuality ballroom.

All of them were barely glanced at by either the Syld or Mondegreen. The objects were placed on the bed and ignored as they spoke, pleasantly, on no subject that seemed relevant to ending the war. Neither of them showed fear or anxiety, after that first object. They could have been taking tea together, at a fine café.

Beck's frustration grew, as did my own. Sometimes I felt like an object myself, brought to the pinnacle by some arcane request, only to be invisible to those in charge. But there were other times when the emotion of intense connection overwhelmed me, and I felt vital to this process of communication. I was not only their witness but a conduit. Everything they said flowed through me, and was changed by that movement. I had feelings so deep that I would wake to find myself weeping.

*　　*　　*

WE MIGHT HAVE continued indefinitely in such a manner, but delicate balancing acts always end.

The heat of midsummer was approaching. It was early morning, and I had made my usual way to the twelfth floor. It was obvious that nobody else came to this room, so I never bothered to pack anything away. Surrounded by the detritus of Droad, I leaned into the crates and scattered one broken, useless treasure after another across the floor, disturbing the dust as I wished.

One crate, near the back of the room, had contained part of a design that I recognised. The coat of arms for the owners of Vella Iffluce, a great house in the centre of the city, was an unfolding fern above the nest of three baby birds, and the design had been stamped into every keystone of the many archways. When one surfaced in the crate I recognised it instantly. I had admired that fine building many times, set in stately public gardens, with tall marble pillars and an ornate portico. I dragged the crate towards the window, the better to see the contents in natural light, and turned it out.

Rubble. Twisted pots, broken plates. The usual. But at the bottom—a glint of something more interesting. I leaned in and retrieved a necklace. Not a precious one, but a cheap example that reminded me of the trinkets they used to sell in the market, aiming to attract those who wished to emulate the rich. It was an evocative object for me. My mother had owned a small box in which she kept three such necklaces, and she picked which one to wear depending on her mood, every morning. I had not cared for her offer to choose one to be given as a present to me, even though they were dear to her. I'd turned her down without thinking of whether my rejection of what pleased her would hurt her feelings. I had thought such objects beneath me, once I'd begun to be tutored in better things. Now I held that retrieved necklace as if owning one had long been a dream of mine.

How odd, I thought, *that meanings and desires are changed,* and as I straightened up and held the necklace against my throat I looked out of the window to find a perfect day, the water a blue-green smooth expanse, the sky emptied of all but golden sunshine. Yes, summer was here, and the future with it. I could see the harbour of Stravatch with such clarity.

Boats.

Not the circular boats of fishers, not the long thin canoes of traders. Boats of war in stages of construction, and others already made, ready to bear many bodies across the lake. The enemy had been hard at work under the cover of the cloud and smoke.

There could be no doubt. They planned to come for Crag.

CHAPTER SIXTEEN

"They come for Mondegreen," said Pappas.

"No doubt." Imberley blew on the top card of the deck, and turned it over. Ten of knives. "Damn." She threw her hand onto the pile. "He's their symbol, their delight, and we stuck him in the pinnacle. That inspires them to acts as ridiculous as marching to save him."

I thought of him: as the man on the high wire, the man in the box, the man caught. He no longer inspired me; that would have required a distance I no longer felt. Maybe the closer the enemy came to Crag, the less they would idolise him.

No. No, that did not seem probable. They wanted to reach him, touch him, carry him triumphant from the highest room of Crag. Another high-wire act, after all.

"He's a legend for a reason," said Pappas.

"But shouldn't his reputation of genius rely on his ability to escape without their help?" Imberley asked, as she dealt another hand. The cards had been procured in trade—given in exchange for an extra meal by one of the survivors of Stravatch—but the games did not favour her as the dice often did. I was relishing this change of fortunes. It was not that the cards often fell my way, but the sheer amount of variables in play made me think that one day they might.

"Starke thinks it's a show of force, nothing more," said Tommo, glumly. He played a Mutuality card. A strong start.

"You'd rather they attacked," said Pappas. He played a three, effectively ending his hand in the game. He had no hopes of winning this one with the cards dealt to him, then.

"I've volunteered for outside duty if they do," said Tommo.

Imberley laughed. "You'll stand on the beach and go toe to toe with them? What purpose would that serve? I'll be safely behind the gate, and so should you be, Tommo. Save your heroics for a battle you can win."

"Let them try me. I'll take them all on," Tommo said. He had never sounded younger.

"I'm sure you will," soothed Pappas. "I have every faith in you." The words disgusted me, for some reason I could not name. I threw down my own cards and rose from our current spot by the courtyard gate. It was late, well after sundown; the courtyard was emptied of all but a few. I had thought it a blessing to find time in the schedules when we were all free, but in the days since we had all placed our bets together, I had changed. The meetings with Mondegreen and the Syld were altering me.

"Jan!" called Imberley. I ignored her. I made my way to the barracks, and slept badly. Perhaps everyone did. I could not imagine that there was a person who had not thought it through, attempted to do the calculations in their heads: how many troops would be needed to overwhelm us? How many would die?

I had longed for battle. Now it was coming to me, and I wanted to run away.

"WE ARE RUNNING out of time," said the Syld.

She sat in her usual seat, her hands clasped in her lap. She projected a calmness at odds with her words.

"What would you have me do about that?" Mondegreen asked, his tone as mild as her own. He shifted position on the bed, tucking one ankle up under his thigh, then reached out and touched the item I had retrieved from the twelfth floor that morning. A small wooden box, rectangular, without pattern: the lid scarred and burned, but intact. He flipped it open, exactly as I had done only an hour earlier, and found— nothing. It was empty. "Sometimes there is the promise of meaning, but that promise, once explored, is so much smaller than expected."

"I don't understand you," she snapped, her temper rising from nowhere, and he smiled; he had managed to get under her skin.

"You did once. You knew me so well you could read my mind."

"No, mind-reading has ever been one of *your* parlour tricks, Marius. You were very good at it."

"I gave that impression."

"Isn't that the same thing? You fooled me, early in our friendship. You conjured, and refused to be bidden, and I was impressed enough to think well of you. Do you remember?"

He closed the lid of the empty box. "I remember that we were alike, you and I."

"And so we are."

"No," he said. "Not anymore."

"We agreed, did we not, that we wanted the end of this war? Do you no longer want that?"

An expression, maybe regret, passed over his face, as sad and slow as a song. "It isn't my own motives that I doubt."

She pushed backwards, the legs of her chair scraping against the floorboards. "I'm hurt," she said. "You have hurt me." There was disbelief in her voice, and pain. "If you continue to wound me, Marius, I will not be at my best for what lies ahead of us."

"And what does lie ahead?" he asked.

"We go around in circles. You're the mind reader. Read the

minds of those outside this room, and tell me what you see there."

"I see an end."

They looked at each other. Without playfulness, without artistry.

She broke their shared gaze casually, turning away from him. I sucked in a loud breath: a sound that I was certain they both heard, and both chose to ignore.

That they had no choice but to ignore.

CHAPTER SEVENTEEN

DEFENCE DRILLS STEPPED up in pace, taking up the afternoons, and we were divided into two groups: those who prepared for an onslaught, and those who took up the onus of menial duties. I was between the two groups: exempt at times, yet still expected to answer the call of those that commanded me. The area guards now all knew that I had been given leave to come and go as I wanted. They barely seemed to see me anymore as I exercised my freedom to wander, which was the strangest of sensations after years of strict abidance of the main principles of Crag: run by routine, and stay solely within your role.

I could feel a change in every place I visited.

It was as if there were no longer prisoners and guards but one group, divided into tasks that benefitted the whole. Everyone dreaded the arrival of the force who had destroyed Stravatch, even those who should have been on their side. Some of them asked me: *Are they coming? What will they do? How will this end?*

It did not say much for their side, I thought, that fear was the reaction of the very people they came to liberate. But it was not the many prisoners who were my focus, but the one.

My meetings with Warden Beck returned to his office, as the allotments were now permanently occupied. Tarklow admitted me with his usual quizzical look. One time he even enquired after my health, although I felt he really wanted to say something else entirely. My own words moved further and further from imparting the atmosphere of growing dread and estrangement I found in Mondegreen's cell. The tension between the inmate and the Syld was as fine and delicate as spider's silk, and I felt ever more like the insect caught between them. I was afraid to move, to so much as breathe, for setting all alarms jangling.

The pinnacle was not alone in an atmosphere of anxiety: the austere clarity I had found in Beck's office during our first visit was gone, replaced with piles of documents upon his long desk, and scattered on the floor around. The fireplace housed only a thick layer of grey dust that gave the air an acrid scent, and one corner of the room had been given over to what I first took to be a pile of scrap. It was only after a few meetings that I made sense of it; a broken plate leapt out at me, and I realised it was a collection of the items I had taken, one by one, into Mondegreen's cell. Heaped together, they conveyed no more meaning to me than they had apart. The warden's eyes often turned to them as I stood in front of his desk and gave my report on the day's conversation. A formality returned to our dealings, but I knew his face well enough to see his own worries about Stravatch written upon it.

At the end of one meeting, held late at night, he dismissed me as usual and, as I turned, he muttered, "No time, no time left." I wished he had not embarked upon this habit of talking to himself. He was the very symbol of solid resistance, eternal standing. He could not crack, even an inch, or we would surely all fall.

On the way out, my eye alighted on a small painting, hung by the door, faded in a gilt frame. Delicate strokes of a brush had created an image of Beck, standing proud in his dress uniform: the young war hero, adorned with his chest of medals. How grand and clear and marvellous he looked. I both envied and pitied him, to have that moment of glory in his past, the fear of the battle behind and a clarity of purpose easier to find.

In the corridor, Tarklow waited to be admitted.

"A new object every day," he said. "We all face challenges. These are opportunities to learn." It did not make much sense to me, and I thought he would speak more, but instead he shrugged, a fluid gesture, then turned to the side so I could squeeze past him.

"Thank you," I said.

He acknowledged me with a dip of his sharp chin, then sailed past with an armful of further papers—to add to the pile, no doubt. I closed the door behind him, and felt a prickle of awareness. Someone was watching me.

"Here," called a voice, softly, and I saw the Syld, just visible in the glow of the corridor lamp, the door to her quarters cracked to present a slice of her features.

HERS WAS A plain room of a decent size, with a postered bed and a chest of drawers. She shut the door behind me, and we were alone for the first time.

She was in pyjamas, good linen, striped, buttoned up high. Her feet were bare on stone, which must have been freezing cold; I wondered that she had not made up the fire.

"I prefer the cold," she said. That made sense, after her time spent in the far north.

A pearl-handled hairbrush sat upon the chest of drawers, and next to that, the brooch of the oster. A wooden tray held the remains of her dinner: a smear of gravy, and a piece of gristle that had managed to resist the fork and meatknife that lay in parallel upon the plate.

The famous fur of the Allynx was not on display. I wondered where she kept it.

"Elize," she said. She stayed by the door, and I stood by the bed, unsure whether to even dare to meet her gaze. I had spent hours in her presence, listening to her voice. This was different. "I wanted to thank you for your help. Your presence in that room is... calming."

If she had known me at all she would not have found me so, and for a moment I relaxed. I had kept myself well hidden from her penetrating gaze. Then she said, "It concentrates him upon the telling of stories, you see." So she did not find me serene company herself; she talked of Mondegreen.

"It does?" I asked. My voice emerged too loud for the room, and squeaky.

"Are you not aware of how completely you are in his attention? And that fact soothes me more than I can say. He has not lost his will to entertain, and so he has not lost his desire to amaze, to astound. To escape. He will try to escape. And when he cannot, he will be broken. He will stop telling stories, and he will tell the truth, for the first time in a long time."

She crossed the room, inches from me, and sat on the bed, tucking her small feet up under her. It was an uncomfortable mirror of Mondegreen's own actions—the way he sat, so upright, upon his own narrow bed. They were opposites that had somehow pulled so far apart that they met again, and were shaped by the force of each other.

"Sit down," she said. She patted the bed.

I obeyed her. Not because it was an order, but because it was an invitation, and there had been so few of those in my life. Being seen by her, talked to directly, was as strong as a glamour. I perched there, very still. I was now the object from Droad, chosen randomly, moved casually, for her to turn over in her hands.

"You're very young."

"Not so," I said. "I'm twenty-four."

"My mistake, then," she said, playfully, as if admonished. "You have the look of one both open and secretive, urgent and careless. I see it sometimes, in the very young who have seen too much and not enough."

"Not so," I repeated. I could not bear to be judged in a way that sounded like an easy dismissal.

"I've misread you? I'll tell you something; I'm not guessing. I've read your file. You were in Droad. Your mother was killed. Everyone you loved was killed. You were not present through sheer chance. Then you signed up, immediately, with passion. You spoke in your interview of wanting revenge, but you did not find a way to seek it at the front. You transferred to Crag. Since then, you've done precisely what you've been told to do. You have a reputation for quiet fairness among the prisoners. You're not cruel, or malicious. You don't take out your need for revenge upon them. I think you're waiting. I'm guessing you've yet to make sense of who deserves to feel your wrath, but this war feels senseless to you."

It was too clear a vision of me, too much to bear. I cleared my throat. Greatly daring, forced into action, I said, "This war is not senseless to you?"

ALIYA WHITELEY

She smiled. "I respect your need to understand what has happened. To you alone, and to all of you who fight. I cannot give you any answers. Wait—I can give you something. I can tell you not to trust, nor blame, Mondegreen. Don't trust his stories. They are aimed at your heart. They are... slippery."

"Lies?"

"Not exactly. And not exactly truths."

I tried very hard to remain expressionless, but I could feel my muscles stiffen, my eyebrows draw together. He had told me at least one memory in that cell, exactly as I remembered it. I did not know if I should tell her that, defend him. But she knew him better than I ever could.

"For example," she said, and shifted a little closer to me, "The giving of the coins. The small child who receives his bounty as a retribution upon the rich and greedy of this world."

I could not have borne it if she had tried to claim it as a lie. "That happened," I said. "It happened."

"You heard it as one thing. A wonderful moment. May I?" She put a hand on my upper back, between my shoulders, a very light touch, but I felt it. Her hand moved down my back, tracing my spine through my uniform, my belt, then returning to my collar and beginning a downward path again. "He has performed that trick in every village, every town, every city. He has blessed hundreds, if not thousands, of youths with his stolen coins. He knew you identified him for Beck; he gambled that you were one of them. Think of yourself, as all of you, as an insurance policy—a group, spread wide, none of you knowing the other. But any one of you could be bent to his will when he needed it most. Beware what you hear, for it is not exactly what he says. He is the Misheard Word. That's what his name means."

I sat in silence and let her stroke me, as if I was a great pet, a cat, and we would only ever have each other for company. With every movement of her hand I felt she marked me, and I could not find a way to resist.

CHAPTER EIGHTEEN

IN THE EARLY hours of the morning I left her room. I could not hide. There was no way to evade the usual guard, at the stairwell, who would no doubt report our assignation to Beck. I walked past with my eyes on the ground, feeling a blush on my cheeks. Why did I feel robed in guilt? I was a free person. And yet, when she had brought forth the thick white fur of the allynx from her chest of drawers, and bid me lay down, covering me, asking me to close my eyes for a moment in her company, I had felt compromised. Bound to her. Even though I felt sure that she had lied to me, too. They were both liars, in their own ways.

I had dozed off, I think, for the shock of the cold hit me hard when she'd pulled the fur from me. "Time to go," she had said, dismissing me. She had not even wished me goodnight.

And what did I wish for?

I wished I was a child again.

I wished for my mother, who lived a life of cookery, by recipes she knew by heart, knowing how to be happy with what she had.

I wished for Fider, who taught me that there could be more.

I wished to have no inkling of the kind of games adults liked to play, from dice to cards to betting on love, life, and the deaths that must follow.

I wished to be safe inside a home that could not possibly fall.

I wished to be too little to be of interest to the world at all.

I was being used in many ways, by many people. I realised that. Told how to act, how to keep silent to suit their plans. She had stroked me into submission and covered me with her will; she wanted to tie me to her cause, keep me away from the influence of Mondegreen. Why? I descended the stairs slowly, lost in thought.

The kitchen was never quiet. The bakers were already at work, kneading dough by lamplight, in unison, and the smell of the day's bread was escaping from the row of ovens. It was evocative, welcome to me. I had worked the dawn shift in the Mutuality more than once, charged with the preparation of breakfast. Cured meats and fresh fruits had been laid out on bright clean dishes. But my favourite part had always been the bread. Droad had favoured square loaves with tucked corners, each like a pillow. Here, small black rolls scattered with seeds would emerge from the ovens for the lower ranks, one for each of us.

"Not ready yet," called one of the cooks. I straightened, and smiled back at them all. They were a pleasant sight. "You woke with an appetite, soldier? Or do you fancy a shift in the kitchen for a change?"

All I wanted at that moment was to belong to them. I unbuttoned my jacket and rolled up my sleeves, and they whistled and roared and made space for me by the bench. They passed me flour, yeast, a peck of salt. My hands remembered an old expertise, and I fell into their rhythm, making bread. Like my mother before me: making bread for the day ahead.

By the time the last batches were ready, the servers had woken and prepared the crockery. The rolls were placed on long trays and carried off. The prisoners and the refugees came last, and as the final trays were filled, the head cook came to me, and thanked me for my work.

"You can come back any time," he said, as if I could switch jobs so easily, and gave me two warm rolls to take away. I pocketed them, and left the kitchen behind. I knew where to go next, and had to hope that luck was with me for a change.

WHO COULD HAVE foretold it? I was blessed. Fider was in the allotment, tending his patch in the back row, and only a few others were there—most of them having opted for breakfast first, I reckoned. I made my way to him, and held out the spare roll.

"Here," I said.

He leaned on his hoe and thanked me, as if no time had passed, and he had never refused to be in my company. "Bright dawn," he said, and it was.

"Your patch is coming on well."

"The ground is too hard." He bit into his roll, and we ate together in silence. He threw the final bite, covered in soil from his hands, over the fence. "What might seem a waste for one is a blessing for another. I've seen a mousle out there, searching for scraps, and a struggle seen must be either addressed or ignored. Do you remember the lesson of inequality?"

The response came to me automatically. "Inequality is not a fixed state of being. It is a choice." We had examined facets of the world through many disciplines together, looking for connections between literature, philosophy, politics, mathematics. Even history and geography: we had discussed how our cities had been built, and by whom. Where to make that first community, how to manipulate terrain and encourage settlers to destinations—these were the issues at the bedrock of a successful society. We had covered the first split to the north, and the ways of the mountain people who had decided to live there, separate from the accumulation of wealth for the few over the many, and he had stressed how we were yet alike, even though we had fought wars over hundreds of years: the bloodless kind, apart from notable exceptions.

Fider had encouraged me to question all that simply seemed to *happen*, on a natural plane. His words had given me the belief that I could see the patterns of life and tweak them to suit. I would not be a worker in the Mutuality forever, no matter my little birthright, my lack of connection. I had believed him right up to the moment when Droad was destroyed; whatever power I had thought I possessed was nothing in the face of that mighty terror.

"Choice," Fider said, to his carrot tops. "Who is the one with power?"

"The one who makes the choice."

"Think on that." I knew these words as a dismissal, so familiar that they brought tears to my eyes. As a child, I would have swallowed that, taken it away, and pondered it for days. But I was no longer a child.

"How did you escape Droad?" I asked him. "Were you given a choice that others lacked?"

"How did *you* escape?"

"I was sent on an errand by my mother. For apples. The market was sold out, so I walked out to the orchards, and the day was warm, and I kept walking. I told myself I would find the best apples lower down in the valley, and I bathed in the river, and fell asleep under a tree. I woke to a light I—I cannot describe—then the wind, so hot. It knocked me out. I don't know how long for. A farmer found me, took me in. We were ill, for a time, all of us. The people who came out of Droad were worse. They all died, too, eventually. They died with their hair falling out... their teeth crumbling..."

"I know it," he said, quietly. But he did not tell me how he survived.

"They said everyone was dead, and I would die too if I tried to return. If I had thought you'd stood a chance, I would have looked for you. I would not have stopped looking for you."

"Who had the choice of that?"

"I did."

He straightened, glared at me. "*You* did. You chose not to act. Not to find out more. You accepted what you had been told about Droad. Which makes me wonder, Elize, if you have made any choices of your own at all." He groaned as he leaned over his patch once more. "If I could choose a younger back, I would. If I could choose to protect you from what is coming, I would do that too; I tried to. I told you not to talk to me, so they could not tie you to me. But it is too late for that now. They are here."

"In Stravatch."

"No! Here. In Crag. All systems of living have their flaws. There is no perfection in the world, not even in the clockwork runnings of Crag, and there is a problem with my belief in choice: are you ready to hear it?"

I already felt lost in his words, unable to follow to the places he would go to, but answers felt closer than they had in months. What else was there to do but try to keep up with him?

"Everything you see," he said, leaning on his hoe, as if we were back in his office, sharing a delight in deciphering and categorising experience, "everything you will ever think, has already been designed to make it easier to take away your choices. I mean this literally. We live in a reality engineered by higher beings to play out certain roles. They are not of our kind. They come from another world. Again, I stress, word for word, this is truth."

At last: something of which I could be certain. He had lost his mind.

"This war is a product of those higher beings," he continued, warming to his subject. "It suits their aims. They wish us to destroy each other, to have more room for the vast fleet of them that have yet to arrive. For now, they remain secret agents, few and far between. But only one would be enough to bring us all down, with their lies and manipulations, their apparently godlike abilities to appear and disappear, shape our thoughts and actions."

Was it the destruction of Droad or Stravatch that had set him on this path of self-delusion? How long had he been harbouring such thoughts? I could not begin to think of a way to lead him back to reason, but at least I could see where this was heading. "You think Mondegreen is one of these... higher beings."

He dropped his hoe, crouched to a dandelion, poised to yank it free. "I know it."

I pictured Mondegreen, unshaven, in his crumpled shirt, sealed in a box, then sitting in the pinnacle. If he had been able to disappear at will, he would have done it already. "I have spent hours in the presence of this man," I said. "He is human."

"Is that so?"

"The Syld sits with him, day after day, and they talk of their past. It is rooted in the familiar."

"A shared past. That makes sense."

"How so?"

"Because she, too, is a higher being." Fider pulled up the weed, exposing its long, hairy root, and said, "Now go, Elize, and think. Think more, and think better. That is all I ever wanted of you."

THERE WERE SO many boxes on the twelfth floor, and too many connections to ever understand the contents.

I had taken too long trying to find the right person to kill, and now Fider—soft, pampered tutor, then drunkard, then evangelical gardener—had showed me what happened to those who obsessed over such concepts. He was mad. And that meant he was unpredictable, in a place that relied on order.

A wild thought came to me, and would not be banished.

I could give Mondegreen an item that he could use: something that could be fashioned into a key, or a weapon. He would take it, leap up, take the Syld prisoner. He would thank me. See me. He would escape, go to the enemy, retreat, and all would return to normal.

No. No, I could not do it. I did not even know if I wanted him dead or saved. Or forever in some locked room, close by, where I could visit him, listen to his stories. It was laughable, really. A laughable ambition.

I reached into a crate and pulled out a long, thin piece of metal that shined a little brighter than the rest, as if it had been polished clean by the destruction. It had no obvious purpose. Like me. It reminded me of the rulers Fider used to keep in his office, back at the Mutuality, for his students to draw lines upon paper. Paper had not survived the attack, of course; I had not come across a single sheet. But the rulers, and the rules of how we delineate and set down the words inside us, remained.

What Fider had said that morning in the garden was not exactly new to me. It was a twisted remnant of a theory I had heard before, among soldiers and prisoners alike, whenever the world was not on their side. It could be a comfort to claim that choice was an illusion, that all was controlled and would never favour the little people. Some great all-knowing giant who lived in the sky—others muttered of grand plans laid by green lizards. Ridiculous. It was the kind of self-centred philosophy that the Fider I once knew would have despised.

He had encouraged responsibility for one's own actions, commitment to a clear head. Dedication, not abdication.

And yet, for all that his words had sounded like a more detailed variant of an old scapegoat reserved for the bitter and beaten down, he had sounded far from defeated. He possessed an energy I had not seen in him before. This was not philosophy to him. It was reality.

Think, he had told me.

Mondegreen and the Syld, in collusion.

I pocketed the length of nondescript metal to bring to the cell later, then examined the view from the window.

The building of boats continued. Forces were massing.

Fider thought Mondegreen and his kind would rob us all of choice. It was far more likely that such a role would belong to other men, their eyes turned to Crag. And as for the Syld: she had touched me, and her hands were soft. They were human. She was real. And if she was similar to Mondegreen, she was also like me, in some way that I could not have described to Fider in a million years.

CHAPTER NINETEEN

MONDEGREEN BEGAN HIS latest story with weariness thick in his voice, like a tired child wanting words with which to draw a veil on the day:

Once there was a man locked in a tall tower on a desolate stretch of coast. A well-meaning hag had kept him there since his youth, for his own good. There was one window, that faced nowhere but out to sea. He thought there was nothing to the world outside. He saw the sea as a vast painting, and the horizon as a line traced by the steady hand of the hag to amuse him in his loneliness.

Then, one day, a stream of rich carriages passed by the tower. A newly crowned king was on a journey to see every inch of his kingdom. He called for his own coach to stop, and the courtiers in attendance followed suit in their own coaches. The king rolled up his trouser legs and waded out to sea until he could see the one window, high up, in the circular wall of the tower.

He called up, "Who lives here? Who has built upon this land?"

There was a long silence.

The king tried again, and again, and on the third call the man appeared at the window, ashen-faced, terrified. He called down, "I do not know anything but this, my home, and I do not know you. You cannot be real."

"You do not know your own king?"

"What is a king?" called the man.

Astonished, the king shouted, "Do you not wish to come down from this tower and find out?"

"There is only a painting," replied the man, "What good is that? And I must be imagining you. Go away."

"If you were dreaming me up, could you not banish me at will?"

The man's face reflected profound disquiet. He pulled his head back from the window and would not answer to further summons.

The king waded back to shore and considered the situation with his courtiers. It would not do to be unrecognised and disbelieved. They settled on a course of action. A great architect was summoned, and many workmen brought to that stretch of coastline. Building commenced. At the end of a year, a magnificent tower stood in the sea, somehow staying upright, with its roots deep in the sand. It dwarfed the tower built by the hag. It had only one window, facing the one in the first tower, raised slightly above it, so that the man would have to look up at it every day. The king took his place within, and stayed there for the rest of his life, shouting his superiority at the man from morning until night. The king had no view of the painting of the sea, or the line of the horizon, and he did not miss them much.

I wanted to ask what a king was.

They shared this knowledge. Perhaps a king was like a Syld: a figure of power. And what were courtiers? Those who served their country? Would I have been a courtier, back when I worked at the Mutuality, cleaning up, serving others? There was another way of seeing the world here, and a language that went with it.

Mondegreen had not even glanced at the gleaming length of metal, beside him, on the bed. It did not interest him at all.

I looked at the Syld closely. Her fine hands were in her lap, her eyes turned to the point of the ceiling above. She wore the oster brooch again, this time on the right side of her utilitarian dress.

Something she had said came back to me, from weeks ago, when this had seemed to be a meeting of minds I could witness and understand.

The Allynx, the Oster, and the Misheard Word.

There were not two of them. There were three. Whatever they were, there were three of them.

I wanted to stand, to go to her. To shake her, and him, shout at them until they told me something I could comprehend. I was sick of them both, and their stories. I was desperate to know what came next. What would they say next?

The Syld cleared her throat. "It's time to dismantle the tower," she said.

No TIME FOR thought, for sleep, for reason: only ingrained response. My hands shook. I struggled with my buttons, left the top one undone. I found my jacket, ran my fingers through my hair. Around me, others did the same. The bell sounded on, on, loud in the hour when all should have been silent.

To the armoury, in the basement, between the storerooms and the boilers. I waited in line to collect a rifle. I was given one of the older ones, and would have to hope it worked. The mechanism had been greased, and I took that as a good sign. I slung the small pouch of ammunition from my belt. We had drilled for this. I found my way to my appointed post: the courtyard, the gate to the main hall. Pappas would be in the lower prisoner levels. Imberley on the battlement, with a view over the lake. I wondered what she could see, up there: how many were heading this way? The black water, bristling with boats. Moving fast, churning up waves. The front line, a lauded position, would be down at the jetty, awaiting them, Tommo among their number. They would hold back the enemy for as long as they could, firing from the beach. They would engage those that landed, and try to exhaust them. The longer it took the enemy to organise camp, the better; we had the advantage in drawn-out warfare. As long as we could see them approach the main gate we could shoot them down. We had to last out this first night, and make it to the dawn.

Crag has never fallen.

My comrades would take strength from this, beside me, breathing out plumes of air in the unseasonably cold night. I knew why it had not fallen, and why that could not save us.

I had my place in the line, before the door that led to the hall. *I will not be moved. I will not move.*

But a city had been wiped out with one blast. It was possible higher beings walked among us, disguised, impervious. No, no, I could not think that way. I would drive myself mad. I clung to things I knew, and to my rifle, and I pictured Tommo outside the gate, waiting to die in the name of honour.

Honour: I could not find it in my uniform, badly buttoned, nor in the frantic breaths of those beside me. I could not find it in myself at all.

Tommo was out there to die. He had volunteered for it. Had he known that, or was he in denial, picturing some different future, an endpoint in which he ended up painted on a wall, with a chest of medals? We should not have soothed him, played to his fantasies. I felt sick.

Think.

The enemy could not use the weapon that had made a crater of Droad.

They wanted Mondegreen liberated. That meant they had to leave us intact, at least, until after he walked free.

The bell stopped ringing.

I heard my own breath, once, dragged in, and the cannons fired.

Our line jerked, as if we were the ones shot; I felt a sharp pain in my mouth, and my spit was thick, too thick to swallow. I retched. Turned my head away from the line as a black, viscous liquid oozed out of me. Blood, just a little blood, I had bitten my tongue. It felt swollen, alien, in my mouth. I wanted to see if the cannons had hit their mark. Ships, sinking. The enemy in the water, scattered, screaming, drowning.

My job: to hold.

I would hold.

The cannons fired again. We jerked, we waited. Again.

"Hold," called a voice, outside the main gate. "Hold!"

Then:

"Fire!"

Waves of gunfire, on and on, swamping all sound. I could picture it. The lake, alight. Smoke, flame, bodies, wreckage. But more boats coming, more than the cannons could sink, drawing closer, and our guards firing on those that made it to the shingle, pouring forth, beginning their charge up the beach. Tommo shooting. I could imagine him, handsome, firm in his resolve, reloading with a calmness, his hands unshaken. The first line would hold. It was as if the main gate had become transparent to me. The enemy, in such numbers, getting closer, closer, until Tommo had to throw down his rifle, ammunition spent, and draw a knife—

"Open!" screamed a voice, close. Behind me. "Open!"

I would not move.

"Open, open, open!" It was coming from the inner gate that led to the hall. Where the refugees were kept. Someone was pounding upon it, from the inside.

I glanced to my left, my right. I did not recognise anybody in my line; their faces were contorted, unfriendly. How could I have lived among these people for so long and not paid attention? I saw uniforms, that was all. I wanted to say someone's name, speak to them. Pappas. Imberley with the cannons. Tommo.

Fider.

I broke the line. I stepped back, removed the bar across the door. A force barrelled into it, threw it back, and I staggered. Faces loomed at me, more people I did not recognise. I could not make out what they were saying, at first, then it came to me. *Help.* Did they need aid? No, they were joining the line, standing with us. Helping us. Many of them, ready, willing.

I could understand it. It was worse to lie in the dark, only listening, not knowing what would come. Having no sight on whatever came next.

I ran into the hall, heard many moan—did they think me the enemy? "Friend," I called, "Friend," as I looked for Fider. The cots had been turned on their sides, stacked, to form barricades, and people huddled behind them. I shouted his name, asked for him. He was not in the room.

Think. They would want Mondegreen out before destroying us.

Some weak point, some secret opening. Someone from outside, brought in under desperate circumstances. Like the sacking of Stravatch.

A traitor.

It could not be Fider, I would not doubt him in such a way. Not Fider, my tutor, the man who believed in higher powers. Where would he have gone?

I still had my freedom. The guards knew it. They let me out of the side door, to the kitchen. It was emptied of staff; they would be below, with the stores. The room was very cold, the ovens unlit. Unnatural. I took the back stairs at speed, made it to the ninth floor. From the standard cell block, low risk prisoners, I could cut across to the higher ranks' staircase, and climb to the pinnacle. Those inside the cells begged to be let out: some voices were calm, others were frenzied. They promised to fight for us, to defend Crag. At the far end of the corridor, one woman reached through the bars of her cell, fingers closing on air as I passed, and said, very clearly, as if perplexed, "But I'm not with them." All definitions of friendship and enmity were being eroded as this war went on and on. This night somehow held the power to sweep them away altogether, if only it could be unlocked.

It did not matter. None of us could be released.

I did not slow down when I hit the higher ranks' staircase. My lungs burned, my legs threatened to give out. The guards looked nervous, but did not challenge me. When I reached the ante-room the two on duty recognised me and lowered their rifles; I had the sudden realisation that luck was with me, oddly, for this act of running around at speed on a night when even the mildest surprise could have led to a slip of a finger on a trigger. But Beck's dominance over Crag had stayed true; I was to be admitted anywhere, at any time. What an unknowing gift he had given me.

"The cannons have stopped," one guard said.

I thought of telling him that the enemy was on the shoreline, that we fought hand to hand to keep them from the main gate. What good would it do? I nodded.

"He's secure," said the other guard. "Is the Syld coming?"

Of course. They only knew me as an attaché of the Syld. Why would I be here without her?

"I've been told there's a possibility of an attempt at escape," I said. "I'm meant to set eyes on him myself. Warden's orders."

They accepted it, and unlocked the door. Entering that familiar room, knowing those curved walls, was like the final throw of the dice in a long game.

I would have bet all my wraps of hot pepper for a year that he would not be there.

A vanishing act: a final flourish of escape. That was who Mondegreen was. I had already told him goodbye, in my mind. I wished it, deep down. *Let him be gone. Let him be a creature of legend, and let this all be a memory I tell in years to come, if I escape too.*

I was right.

The room was empty.

The bed was made, the sheet pulled tight. Mondegreen's old clothes, his shirt and trousers, lay on the floor, like a skin he had shed. The wind gusted through the window, ripped around the curve of the wall. It was colder here, high up, close to the top of the sky.

I looked out over the view. I could see nothing, no sign of how it was done. No rope, no way to walk out, balance, somehow drop without injury. The night was very dark, and the lake black, and unknowably deep. There were no more ships to sail.

CHAPTER TWENTY

BECK'S OFFICE HAD become a scattered mess, with papers sprawled over his imposing desk, and the carpet. Something had hit the wall by the door, hard—a few of the framed paintings had fallen, their glass fronts smashed. Others hung on at skewed angles. The heap of objects from Droad remained in place, and next to it: Tarklow. Tarklow, laid out, on the floor, a rifle beside him.

I went to him, knelt. He had fallen face down, his long arms and legs straight, as if he had no idea of what hit him; one of the sharp meatknives from the kitchen still protruded from his side. There was little blood. I felt at his neck, above his stiffly starched collar, for a pulse. Nothing. He was still warm.

I saw it, close to where he had fallen: the Syld's brooch. The oster. It lay on the floor. I picked it up.

"It was not meant to be this way," she said. Her voice was very clear, very close, but I could not see her. I left Tarklow's body, moved around the desk. There she was. Sitting with her back against the wall, the unbarred window above her. The Allynx fur was around her shoulders, and the lapel of her grey dress had been ripped back, the material hanging, stained with blood. Tarklow's, and her own. The pallor of her face and the way she breathed, snatching at the air: her hand, pressed to her stomach.

"I'll get help," I said.

"Too late." She closed her eyes. There was such pain in the smallest of movements. She opened them again, and I saw her will, her strength. "Come here."

I went to her, and she took my hand in her own, and squeezed it very tightly. It was slick with blood. "You were to be here sooner," she said. "Only a minute sooner. It would have distracted him. Where did you go?"

"The pinnacle."

"Ah. So you are Mondegreen's, after all. And I tried so hard to bind you to me. That was our plan. Office, then the pinnacle, then the allotments. The order was important. All things in order."

Her voice was weakening. I said, "Save your breath, and I will find a doctor. Where is your injury?"

"He shot me," she said, with a half-laugh, in disbelief. "Who would have thought it? He was never the type for action. We knew he was searching for something, trawling the ruins. Having crates shipped here. We used you to force his hand. He had to check what you selected. Just in case. Just in case."

"Who?"

"The Oster."

"Beck?"

She shook her head. "...arklow." She missed the T, drew the word out strangely, shuddered, and I wrapped my arms around her, tried to hold life within her.

"He attacked you. You defended yourself." I could see it; her desperation, her realisation that I would not come in time— she burst into the room, she confronted him—

She laughed, and the sound contained air, and blood, bubbling. "We were here for him."

"I don't—"

"Revenge," she said, simply, and she died.

"No," I said.

She had covered me with her fur, tried so hard to win me over. I could not bear to close her eyes. I left them open.

I heard shouting in the hallway. The guards who had believed me when I said Mondegreen was still in the pinnacle—could it be them, raising a fresh alarm? They would rush inside, demanding to know why I was here, why I hadn't told them of his disappearance. And they would find Tarklow and the Syld.

I sat with her.

Nobody came.

Beck was elsewhere, down at the main gate, maybe, or in the courtyard, leading the way. Standing where the fighting was fiercest, like a hero.

I had to move. Could not be found here. They would ask questions I could not answer. They would think me involved, responsible. To leave her, the life barely fled from her. I could not. I could not.

I took one edge of the fur in my hands and her body slipped forward, as if it was mine to take, so I did. It was so soft. I held it to my chest, and bid her goodbye. Collected my own rifle. Managed to stand. Managed to walk away.

The corridor was empty. Had all the guards been called to the courtyard? Was Beck, or Crag itself, in danger? I followed the sounds back to the kitchen, through the hall where the young and old cowered. My line stood firm, swollen with additional troops, and Beck was there, commanding, indomitable. I saw the way they all watched him, including the refugees, taking strength from his strength. Tommo's great gesture had failed; it was not yet dawn, and the enemy was at the gate. Crag might fall.

I turned away. My presence would make no difference. Nobody had even noticed my absence. I was, as ever, invisible.

THE ALLOTMENTS LOOKED deserted.

It was only as I continued walking through the crops, the

sweetcorn and beans grown high, that I saw him, at the back, at the small shed that held the tools. A man in uniform.

Mondegreen.

He turned; I realised I must have said his name aloud. I could not see his face clearly, and then he was gone, vanished, a vision that clears in a moment. I ran through the crops, trampling them, pushing them from my view. No, he was gone, without trace, once more. It was his fame, his nature.

The floor of the shed was wooden. I noticed one section was not quite flush. I put my fingers to it and it rose in one piece, to form a trapdoor. Beneath it was a larger opening, soil scraped away, to reveal within a curved section of metal under the ground—an outflow pipe? Of course, washing water usage had been limited for weeks now; waste levels would be low enough inside for someone to crawl through.

I knelt. The stench of human waste was overpowering. The longer I waited, the further away he got from me. I dropped my rifle, clutched the fur to my chest. Leaned over, held my breath, crawled inside. The trapdoor closed behind me, and left me in blackness, filth.

I moved forward.

WHEN I EMERGED from the other side of that tunnel, after some length of time I could name as neither moments nor months, I stood in a tiny cove not on any map I had seen.

The skies had cleared. The moon was high and bright in the sky, and Crag was a tall shape back along the coast, jutting from the mountains. In that direction, Lake Haspen was littered with wood, smashed shapes. Shouting and screaming, but far away, and the bell, too, tolling some sort of end.

I waded into the lake, fully clothed, still holding the fur. The cold took my breath. I plunged down deep, feeling the water lift my hair and fan it, feeling it slide between my fingers, my toes, touch me, cling to me, surround me. I stayed there, suspended in the moment of recognition; one life was over. Another was about to begin.

He was waiting for me when I surfaced.

I waded ashore to where he stood, on the shingle. He looked at me, and knew me, and it was what I had wanted, all along. To be seen.

"Here," he said. He pointed to a fresh pile of clothes on the rocks, and I went to them, and began to strip. He did not turn around, and I did not ask him to. I wanted his eyes on me. The white shirt and the grey trousers were a little baggy. But of course, they were not really meant for me at all.

"She's dead," I said, and he nodded.

"I should hate you for that," he said.

"Do you?"

"I'm not sure." He looked away from me, then, and I nearly shouted his name, but it was only for a moment. His attention was upon a shape on the waves. A small boat. It was painted entirely black, from the tip of the sail to the planks, and the movement of the waves made it very difficult to focus upon. "It's a boat for two," he said. "They'll kill you if you stay."

"Who will?"

"Does it matter?"

No, it didn't matter. Friend, enemy. If my own side won they would blame me for his escape, and the murders. If the other side won, they would demand answers I could not give. "Where are we going?" I asked him.

"Droad."

"You mean Chasm," I reminded him. "Droad no longer exists."

He squinted up at the sky. "The end of the night is upon us. If you come with me, I will tell you a story."

He knew exactly what to say to manipulate me, yes, but my awareness of that did not change how much I wanted to be wrapped up in his company. "Will you give me an explanation?"

"Isn't that what I just said?" He looked me up and down. Fully dressed, I felt as if I had stepped into a role previously denied to me. Was I now his companion, his partner? I was no longer the soldier, the guard. I had failed in both of those roles. "If you are coming, come now."

I followed him to the boat, took my place in the prow, leaving my uniform behind. The fur of the Allynx, I took with me. Sopping wet, I folded it and placed it beside me. It would dry in time, and be as soft and beautiful as it once was.

Sticking up from the fold was a small white label, sewn in place, with printed words upon it. While Mondegreen steered us across the lake, following the path in his head to the city that had been destroyed, I read them over and over. They were odd, exotic. Beyond sense, or meaning. Misheard, misplaced, mysterious:

Polyester & acrylic fibre mix
Machine wash at low temperature
Do not tumble dry
Reshape while damp

He began to speak. He said,

BOOK TWO
COSHAM

WORDS, ELIZE, ARE the key to it all; words, and the way they sound inside you, before they come into being, erupt from the cavern of your mouth into the spaces of this wondrous world. The mountains, the plains, so clean, untouched by human invention. Beyond anything I had seen before. The words are different in immaculate air.

Crag is one such word. It has sharp edges, strength, and it feels permanent. Fixed in the time and place of your people. You speak of Crag and everyone knows, agrees with you, bolsters your meaning. Crag is being destroyed, behind us, as we sail away, right at this moment. They said it would never fall, did they not? That doesn't matter. How could it? It remains a fixed entity in your minds: a point around which you can stand as one. Destroyed Crag, ruined Crag, Crag in pieces, these make no difference. We look back on Crag. We leave it behind us, and sail to worse waters.

Crag is the word of this world, for me.

When I think about the world in which I grew up, I say to myself one word: Shitshow.

It doesn't have the grace to be clearly one word or two; even that aspect of its character is a matter of personal choice. It has no meaning set in stone. One person's shitshow is another person's shoeshine: words, strung into phrases, meaning whatever sense anyone wants it to mean. It means nothing to you, of course, and this was all so much easier when I did not have to look in your eyes. You listened, and listened, and I spoke in my slippery way. I let my gift with words take you, claim you. Then I ran away with you; I could not help myself, it always was my game.

Archetta saw the danger, and tried to bring you back, for you were to go to her first, that was the plan. A distraction, at the crucial moment. Help in subduing him. You were to be hers. Nearly everyone was. You did not belong to her, at the last. You arrived too late. But your eyes are so very empty of consequence, your face impossible to blame. I cannot quite read your depth, and being certain a person is shallow is necessary to summon real contempt. How can I hold both concepts at the same time? It was not our intention to bring Crag down, and if I was in this boat with Archetta she would be furious at this outcome. She would call it a shitshow, and I would agree, and we would be united by the place in which we started once more, staring into the collider, before we had to deal with the death and mayhem we unleashed because we are imperfect people from an imperfect world.

I don't expect you to understand this.

There's a different way of living. There's a place that fucked itself until it bled, until it was little more than a violated, catatonic, cannibalised victim of its own intentions, and we came from there, Archetta and I. We found a way up through the mess of it, and our escape was Collision.

The collider had been running for years before I was even born. It was common knowledge by the time I reached secondary school. We had a lesson about it, and it was presented as a magnificent scientific breakthrough: a joint project between the government and private investment that had culminated in a stable observation platform to an inhabited planet with a sustainable approach to resources and social order that we were monitoring, studying for our own long-term good. We were told that answers were coming—that even knowing of the existence of this other world was inspiring our leaders to do better. We should become scientists, and help that change. I remember a recorded scene from a colourful market that looked less than real; I did not take it seriously. Nobody believed anything much, at that age. The only interesting thing about it was its proximity to Cosham. Collision—the private investment company—had built its facility in the Solent, off the coast of Portsmouth, upon a decommissioned aircraft carrier called the HMS *Iris*, and the video we were shown was part of a recruitment drive, as one of the big employers of the area. In fact, my uncle worked there, catching the private ferry from the terminal close to the pier for his shifts. Sometimes he told stories of the great scientists who worked there, the experiments they were undertaking. He gave me a gold coin bearing the face of Newton, a scientist from our shared history; he said it was a commemorative relic, from the past, worth something. I cherished its worn, solid weight.

I liked science, which I think is why he talked to me about these things, but my passions lay elsewhere: history and magic. The two seemed linked to me, somehow. Most days, after school, I cycled five miles to Portchester Castle, and walked around the ancient walls. I would stand on the small jetty, stretching out towards the Spinnaker, and hold out the gold coin, over the murky grey water. I practised my sleight of hand there, tipping the coin between my fingers. If I dropped it, I ran the risk that it would be lost to me forever.

The castle had been a fort first, in Roman times, then the beginnings of a grand castle from Richard II's reign, never finished. It housed prisoners after that, from the Napoleonic wars; they carved their drawings and prayers into the walls. I thought maybe their words protected that place, like a spell. It made no sense. Nothing in my world made sense. Random names, random times, too many things to ever hold in stillness.

I was overwhelmed with expectations and warnings, pleasures, thoughts, and statements: total, consuming sound. It was transmitted through the air itself, and it could not be escaped. I stopped speaking for a while, when I was a child. I would not open my mouth. And I think—although I do not remember this—that I simply did not want to add to the noise that surrounded me. I was taken to see a doctor, and a visit to an ear, nose and throat specialist was booked. She held a metal instrument to my face and I screamed until she took it away, and the voice was recovered. Fear is a great motivator. Finding my voice, losing my coin. These experiences shaped me, so by the time I left education I was mouthy, quick-witted, fast with my hands and feet and sure, between the coin and the words on the walls, that I was protected from the worst of my world. I put my faith in the idea that something would happen to me, something amazing. I would be discovered. It was laziness on my part.

Meanwhile, my uncle worked nights at Collision, and when my parents panicked that I would find no direction after college that had the makings of a real job, they asked him for help.

I don't remember the first time I took the ferry to HMS *Iris*. All I recall of those early days was boredom. I was assigned to security duty outside the collider, and I realised quickly that all it involved was checking the passes of visitors. I say checking passes—in fact, even that was unnecessary. The real monitoring took place on the shore, before the expensive launch left Southsea, and there were cameras everywhere on board, placed above every internal door. Nobody got through to the collider without having been recorded and verified hundreds of times, and I was there only for the show of it. I was the final step before admission, like a bouncer with gold teeth at the entrance to a glitzy nightclub. I had to wear a boiler suit, thick-soled boots and a peaked cap, all in Collision Green; I looked like a fucking idiot from some second-rate science fiction movie. It was a pretence.

My uncle told me that there was a fast-track program for promising young employees: a sponsorship deal which meant one could study part-time at the University of Southampton around shifts. The fees for such courses were exorbitant, and I harboured some daydream of being offered the chance to study history if I promised to work as an archivist or chronicler of Collision afterwards. Many large organisations employed curators to cultivate their historical image, which was code for rewriting the truth of slavery and suffering. All I had to do was show my potential in this area to someone.

But as the days passed it became obvious that there was no-one to show. My line manager had no interest in me, and I could not blame him. I was a chimp in a boiler suit, watching the workers in white coats escort visitors into the holy presence of the collider. They passed by, clipboards clutched to their chests, never acknowledging my existence. The great metal door would swing open, back, and they would step over the threshold, leading the way to a level of knowledge and power I began to realise I would never have.

It took a while before I began to suspect that the workers in white suits were also part of the great show. I caught a glimpse of a clipboard as visitors were ushered through with a wide gesture, and it was blank, shockingly blank and white, and then I wondered—why would a high-level scientist have need of a clipboard at all? Who worked on paper anymore? It was part of a costume, like my thick-soled boots and peaked cap. The collider was meant to be the greatest scientific discovery of all time, and I saw no science. I only saw the parade of pretence, shift after shift.

I tried to talk to my uncle about it, in the cafeteria on the upper deck. I kept my voice low. Why, I don't know. I'd seen too many films; suspected too many conspiracies to count.

"Who cares if it's a show?" he said. "The scholarships are real. For science, mind. Not for stuff that doesn't make money. Waving your hands at people isn't going to get you far. Best get on and do some actual work."

If there had been actual work to do, I would have done it.

I realised then that my uncle didn't like me, and I didn't like him. I found out later that employees got a bonus for each relative they brought into the Collision fold. It made the vetting process easier, apparently, and saved them money. At one point my manager asked me if I had any brothers or sisters looking for work; it was the only time he expressed an interest in me.

Maybe I should have used my sleight of hand abilities to shove the job up his arse.

But I didn't. I was passive. I was raised that way. We all were, in that world. We lived in a hazy web of dreams and distractions, sticky and soft around us. The sound, the sound. Always the sound. God. So many things here you couldn't possibly understand.

I first saw Archetta when she strolled past me in the canteen.

She was wearing the boiler suit, the thick shoes, but the cap was pushed into the belt around her waist and she had brown hair, cut very short. It would be easy to say at this point that she looked like a star, or some other ridiculousness, but it would not be true. She looked like everyone else who worked in security: tired, bored, and wishing they were somewhere else. I don't think I would remember that first glance at all except that she dropped her yoghurt—one of those non-fat ones pretending to be a healthy choice—and it exploded like a bomb beside my table, a great white splat that coated my leg. She said sorry a lot. She was young. I thought maybe it was her first shift. She didn't know where to find serviettes, how to begin to clean up the mess. I wish I could say I helped her, took charge, but trust me when I say it's only that kind of world in dreams. I left her to it, and swiped at the yoghurt with toilet paper in the men's toilets.

Our shift patterns did not cross, and I saw her next months later, at the Christmas party.

It was held in early November, off-ship, in one of those generic business hotels on the outskirts of Portsmouth. Coaches were organised to take employees from Southsea, and there was a free bar up the far end of a long beige room with not enough plastic chairs, and tinsel tied from the fixtures. There was only one type of beer on tap. It was cheap and soapy, and I wasn't much of a drinker. Still, I drank it. I saw her from a distance; she was on the parquet square that was being used as a dance floor, as hits were played by an enthusiastic local DJ who stood behind a flashing deck with a miniature Christmas tree on his head. She wore an electric blue leatherette catsuit. She looked sweaty. She did the Macarena with two other young women, and she did not look out of place. Everyone dressed up for work parties, determined to make the most of it. They lived for those occasions as if it offered a window to a different life, as if they would not need to take painkillers with a pint of water before going to sleep that night. She was laughing and confident. So different from that yoghurt-dropping disaster zone. It had taken only a couple of months to change her. I wondered if I had changed too, and in what way. It was a depressing thought, and I felt weirdly jealous of her. What if she had found something at Collision that I had missed?

On the coach once more, being driven back through Portsmouth at half past eleven, she sat next to me. I had no idea why, at the time. There were many empty seats; I'd chosen one halfway down, avoiding the groups at the front and back, knowing I was over the limit and wishing I'd booked a cheap room in the hotel like many others, although wasting my Christmas bonus on that had struck me as the height of stupidity. I suspected Collision had some sort of deal with the hotel, and I resented the manipulation.

She slid in beside me, on a gust of perfume and perspiration, and said, "Have you got a bottle of water? That gin was rank. I'll have a head on me tomorrow, and I'm on first thing."

"No, sorry," I said, thinking she'd get up, move down the coach. At the back they were quietly, mournfully singing 'White Christmas,' knowing about one line in three.

"Fuck," she said. She slumped backwards in the seat.

Side by side, we travelled for a while, not talking. It was not companionable. I tried desperately to think of something interesting to say while ignoring my insistent bladder. We crossed over the bridge that connected Portsmouth to the mainland, and pulled up at a traffic light that didn't look interested in turning green even though there was no other car on the road.

"I'm Archie," she said. "And you're... Miles?" That was my name back then. "You do the main door, right?"

I nodded.

"I'm up in the suite," she said. She must have seen from my expression that I didn't know what she was talking about. "With the high-class rollers. Not there just for the standard tower. I get them drinks and stuff."

"For the scientists?" I asked.

"Cute."

I couldn't bear to look her in the eye; she was too close, too powerful in her secrets and her scent, her intensity. I trembled at the edge of her. "You know they're not scientists, though, right?" she said. "They're tourists. They come to stare at the other place, see what some world looks like when it's not been cocked up by humanity." She did not sound bitter, or jaded, as she said those words. There was a gleeful, free edge to it, as if she was not responsible, not one of our kind at all. "It's hilarious," she said. "The ones who file past you get to see into the collision for a minute, thinking it's a rare honour, and the ones in the suite are up there every day, for hours."

I thought back to the market scene we had been shown as children: the colours, beyond bright. "Oh, fuck," I whispered, "It's a scam, isn't it? It's all a scam."

"It's real!" she said. She didn't seem to care if anyone overheard. "No, that's the weirdest thing about it, it's real, but what they're all seeing is a live feed through a tiny camera placed high up on a building over there. The actual collisions aren't just stuck out in the open, on either side, I reckon. Didn't you wonder why nobody over there even looked at it? Wouldn't they all be staring at this big hole in the middle of their marketplace?"

"I never thought about it," I said. It was true. I felt as if I was the bystander, and she was the collision; she was a hole that led to thoughts that would have been forever beyond me, without her. Wild, frightening, world-changing thoughts. We were nearly back at the pier.

"How come you know this stuff?" I said.

"Look at me." It was a command I couldn't refuse. I steeled myself, turned a little in my seat, and met her eye. Her blue mascara had clumped her lashes together, and sweat had glued strands of hair to her forehead. It was hard to hold her gaze, keep her in focus. "You're really fucking drunk," she said. "You're not driving back, are you? My flat's only along the seafront. You can have the sofa."

"Thanks," I said, thinking, *I can't believe she really likes me.* I was an arsehole, back then.

We walked along the beach, the edge of the black sea close to our feet, then up the three flights to her flat, in one of those old Victorian piles that used to be grand hotels for people rich enough to take a holiday. She made me coffee and talked on, describing the suite as a room of plush sofas, endless drinks, and betting slips, underfoot, sticking to the thick soles of her shoes as they were discarded at the end of each round—for that was the way Collision made its real money: gambling. The high-end clients bet on the lives of people from another world, trying to predict who might walk down the street that day, and what might be for sale at each market stall. Not big things, life-or-death events. Nothing exciting ever happened on the unnamed street. Archie talked of how boring these perfect lives looked. This was not the level of drama we were all used to. She talked of watching these unexciting events while serving drinks and taking bets, and realising something terrible.

"Our lives have become copies of what we see on TV," she said.

We were imitations of those heightened performances we sucked up all day, every day. It was a language we all spoke without realising it: fiction. Make-believe. In ourselves, in other people. A layer of deceit that cloaked us all, suffocating us, and all we could do was watch the people on the other side of the collider breathe deeply of their fresh, sweet air.

She could be poetic, given free rein, too many gins and a receptive audience.

She talked for hours and I, like an idiot, was flattered. I thought she wanted to be friends, to make me her companion; that this was an outpouring prompted by the adoration in my eyes. Weren't we connecting? Really *connecting?*

She kissed my cheek at about three, and went to bed.

I slept on the sofa, in a camo sleeping bag she retrieved from the back of a cupboard. It smelled of cheap aftershave and I pictured a previous owner, some large Army type. The sofa was old and lumpy, and I woke with a headache and a sore neck.

She was on early shift, and I wasn't. She breezed out of her bedroom in her boiler suit, her short hair wet and spiking, while I was trying to refold the sleeping bag. She said, "Coffee, strong, black, right?" as if she had known my preferences for an age, and it had only slipped her mind. The kitchen was a small alcove attached to the living room, barely big enough for both, so I stood awkwardly by the archway as she moved around the sink, filling the kettle, retrieving cups from an overhead cupboard. The touches of personality she'd added to the flat looked less convincing, a little shabbier, in the morning light: a woven cushion with a fluffy cat's face upon it, a generic print of a woman staring into the sea blu-tacked to a wall. She took a white fleecy throw rug shaped like an animal skin down from the cupboard and threw it over the sofa.

"You're quiet," she said, over her shoulder.

I cleared my throat. "About what you said last night—"

"I know. They're meant to be learning how to make things better."

"Are they?"

"Isn't that what science is?" She came to me, two mismatched mugs in hand, and handed me the novelty one in the shape of Yoda's head. "*Fucked up it is,*" she croaked. "You need paracetamol?"

"Yeah, thanks."

Next to the window was a small desk with a rolltop. I would never have put it down as her style. She opened the drawer and took out a packet of pills. There were many silver rectangles in there, floating on a sea of papers, covered in a free, looping handwriting. Hers, I guessed. "Keep the packet."

"Thanks."

"That's a fiver," she said, her face very straight, and I laughed, then stopped, watching her, looking for clues. Nothing. Serious or joking, I couldn't read her. It was magnificently strange; I hadn't realised how easy I had found other people to read, before that moment. Her blankness created a tension I hadn't felt before, and I could only guess that she was enjoying it. She was dangerous.

I fell back on an old defence mechanism. I took out my wallet, retrieved a note, but did not pass it to her. I kept it close to my body. Her eyes flicked up to mine; I could see her assessing the situation. Her hand shot out, reached for the note. I was faster. The note jumped from my left hand to my right. Her eyes widened, but she was faster than many; she reached again. Gone. I held up my empty hands for her to see, then said, "Look in the drawer."

"Seriously?"

"Look in the drawer."

She opened it with such caution. Her expression was very beautiful to me at that moment; she was so rarely anything other than guarded, but I saw a flash of childlike excitement. Not for the trick, but for the idea she might have been bested. I have thought about it many times since.

"It's not there," she said.

"No. But the paracetamol are. At that price, you can keep them."

She picked them up and gave them back to me. "No, you earned them, you earned them." We exchanged a smile, and something passed between us. Possibly the recognition of an equal. "I have to go," she said, "but I want to talk to you. Meet me later." She named a time and place the following day—a pub I knew close to the Quays—and kicked me out, making it clear she didn't want to be seen together. I stood blinking in the early morning sun, then turned away from the sea and walked into Southsea a little, towards a decent bakery I knew. It was cold, and I was aware of the scent of booze on my clothes, my breath. The shops were just opening: the artisan cafés with spider plants in the window, and the charity shops with black bags piled in the doorways, spilling into the road. The newsagent's stand, bearing the papers, shouted of the latest tipping point breached, targets missed, and an actor in a straight-to-streaming series who had sexted some under-sixteens. There's a kind of nostalgia for a time and place in this that I cannot convey to you. It could never make any sense. Anything can be missed, sometimes, when one is at a distance from it that cannot be covered. How strangely the world of my birth comes back to me, after all this time. That morning, thinking Archie might be a genuine friend, that we had begun something that could transcend who we both were to become bigger and better people: I dreamed this, I floated upon it, over the black bags in the street, and the headlines in the air. Noise, noise, noise.

I was both right and wrong. Being both—that, too, is part of my world. Not yours.

I bought a croissant and a latte, and returned to the seafront, and my parked car, then drove home. I still lived in Portchester, with my parents, and felt a paralysing shame about it, so I did not talk about them—or *to* them, if I could help it. My mother made me a bacon sandwich when I got in, and I didn't thank her. I was very young; I didn't even know it. It shames me to think of them now, but it's too late. Too late to apologise, to be a better son. I thought about what Archie had said to me, and what she might say to me later. When I took the ferry in for my afternoon shift, I saw the *Iris* with changed eyes.

Of course my door, my area, was a grand fake. There was a theatricality about it that I had simply accepted: the thick circular door with many locks and clicking mechanisms; the glass plinth behind which I stood; the lines and arrows painted on the floor. It was an entertaining idea of what a top-secret facility should look like. The tourists filed past it for a look at a projection of the real collision. It was sleight of hand. I understood it. I wondered where the suite was, and how rich a person had to be to buy a stake. There were three worlds on the carrier: that of the workers, that of the rich visitors, that of those in charge of the games. Did Archie know all three? How did she get her information? Was she smiling at them at that moment? I didn't care for the smile. It was her flat stare, that perfectly straight line of the mouth, that I liked. But I realised as I stood on deck, wrapped up in my padded coat over my boiler suit as we approached the *Iris*, I did not like it enough to be controlled by it.

I decided not to meet her.

After my shift I rode the ferry back to the car park and drove home. No—I tell a lie. I drove to Portchester Castle, and walked around the thick walls, looking out over the harbour and the Spinnaker, and the way the lights' reflections were brown and warped by the deep water of the Solent. When it came down to it, being alone was safer.

A week passed. November became December, and the set days off over the festive period edged closer. I had lost all incentive to do well for a scholarship—what was the point if they weren't even doing any science on the carrier? I was part of a giant floating tourist attraction. The world was not going to be saved after all; I knew it, I had always known it. It was an odd relief to be proven right.

I didn't see Archie, and I was glad. It wasn't that I felt detached from her by this distance. In fact, it had the opposite effect; I felt connected to her, by the thread that joins the seeker to the hider. At some point she would come to me, and I wanted that. I would outlast her command. I would make her come.

But she outplayed me.

I received a mail from management. I'd been identified as a candidate with the desired qualities for promotion. Attend a training day, just before Christmas. A room number was given that was unfamiliar to me, and a map. It was different from the ones provided during initial training. The greyed-out areas were replaced with rooms, numbers, complexities that had not been hinted at before, including executive quarters, marketing and publicity spaces, and the suite.

The suite was high in the ship, on one of the upper decks, and the training day was marked for the room next door.

The working days before Christmas are notoriously slow and easy. No major decisions are made, nobody tries their hardest or changes their patterns. They hold, and wait for the break, then return with reluctance in January, and are in a fervour of rushed discontent a few weeks later. Nobody got trained, or promoted, in the last days of December, but as soon as I arrived in that room it was obvious big decisions had been taken about my future. There was no possible way I would have been admitted to that space without pre-agreed clearance.

It was a long space, narrow, with a panoramic window of darkened glass running the length of one side, revealing a view over a much bigger hall, carpeted, with black and white checks; chairs and sofas likewise in monochrome, arranged in artfully informal groupings. A huge screen at the far end, the biggest I had ever seen, showed that same market scene I had been shown since school. It was dark in the other world, with pinpoint lights hanging from the empty stalls in arcs.

The suite, I thought.

Oddly, it looked suitably seasonal.

"Welcome," said a man. He had been there the whole time, standing behind the door, next to a sleek, expensive coffee machine. "You're not late. Thank you." He had a quick, watchful way about him, a tall thin man in a good suit without a tie, the top button of his collar undone. Unobtrusive, probably the one in charge in any room, and never gave it away. "Unfortunately, the other trainees are late. Would you care for coffee? It's a decent brew, actually. I insist upon it for these rooms. One of the perks of being part of the inner circle, if you like." He carried on talking, poured me coffee, kept up an easy dialogue without needing me to take up words at all. It was a skill, and he kept it up for ten minutes, maybe more. We were sitting at the training table, long and slim, with two laptops and notepads positioned ready for use when the other trainees arrived. I was not surprised to see Archie: who else would it have been? She led the way in a group of three; the two behind her were older. One was a man with an explosion of hair and hot blue eyes, with an energy of electrocution about him. The other was a small, self-enclosed woman in a blue cardigan and a dress that swamped her. She took a seat and faded herself into it, as if she did not wish to be visible. We did introductions. Archie, who had slid into place next to me without so much as a glance in my direction, went first. She adopted a strange,

ironic formality as she gave her real name: Alice Higgsley.
She talked of growing up in Cosham, and I knew that was a
lie. It had only one school and I would have remembered her.
Watching her tell an untruth was fascinating. She was very,
very good at it. She raised all the things a person deserving
of a promotion should say, and made them all sound new, as
if she had only just thought of them.

Then it was the turn of the shocked man, keen to speak, fast-
talking and very nervous, for some reason I couldn't fathom:
nerves beyond the situation. Maybe he felt unworthy to be
there. His name was Alex Tee. I couldn't work out how much
of the name given was an abbreviation.

The small woman gave a warm, unremarkable speech, and
it began with her name: Gwen Last. There was something so
fitting about it that I almost snorted, and I felt Archie shift
in her seat, as if supporting her own amusement. I don't
remember much of it. The speech mentioned a degree in
Management Science, I think. We were a mismatched bunch. I
couldn't work out what any of us had in common.

When she had finished, the trainer nodded, as if we had met
some standard for approval. He tapped on the keyboard of
his laptop once, and the whiteboard on the far wall shared a
prepared graphic:

TACTICS AND OUTCOMES
A preparatory course

Designed and delivered by
OTS
Otter Training Solutions
Trevor Arklow CPHR

A small cartoon of an otter, nose curled to tail, making a circle, sat in the bottom right corner.

He began to talk about the world beyond the collision. As he talked, he tapped the keyboard, and new graphics appeared, an entire slideshow laid out, everything agreed in advance. Gwen spread her notebook and wrote things down, phrases such as 'creation of circumstance' and 'plausible deniability.' I felt no closer to understanding what we were there to do.

The first break came an hour and a half later, and I excused myself and used the map to find a bathroom nearby. I looked at my reflection in the mirror for a while. Everything was changing. I couldn't put my finger on how, or why. I felt the cusp of something that would alter me: a designed, strategic happening.

Tactics and outcomes.

I wanted it.

When I emerged from the bathroom she was waiting for me, leaning against the wall, smiling. "You can thank me later," she said.

"Happy to thank you now, if you tell me what I'm thanking you for."

"Haven't you worked it out? I recommended you for this."

Why was it always about who knew who, who recommended who? It was a tiresome business, to think there was no point in being good at anything if all it took was the right friend. And I didn't like her as my superior, so I said, "If you did it as a gift, why mention payment?"

"Is it your birthday, then?"

"No."

"Then why would I give you a gift?" she said. "Naturally, you'll pay me. But I hope it's in a way that surprises me."

We started walking back to the meeting room, in step, side by side. Things were changing. Changing fast. If it meant I owed her, I was open to that—if this opportunity, whatever it was, was as wonderful as she was making out.

The afternoon was filled with the soft drone of Trevor Arklow's voice. In retrospect, I wonder if that was a test itself, to see who could manage to stay awake. He had a cadence, a way of speaking around a subject, using words that pretended to reach for a meaning but were only lazily circling the issues. But I began to see it as its own form of magic trick—a wafting of the hands, a misdirection. He was a conjurer in his own terms, with that lush voice; the subterfuge of administration. Then—wham! Some piece of genuinely astonishing information would be given out, slipped under the audience's radar. Why? I could only imagine that it was a form of safeguarding so that later, when one of us protested as to the nature of the role, he could say *But you were told*, and point to the first time together, in the room, with the view of the suite in plain sight.

Once I had seen the pattern, I could see it coming. And this is what I learned on day one of a training course designed to turn us into infiltrators of your world. I learned that Collision was no longer scientific in intent. I learned that the company was owned by a global firm with a bookmaking arm, and the collider was being run as a high-stakes gambling outfit. And I learned that we were to be trained to have the ability to influence events in the other world to manufacture situations that would encourage interest and investment by patrons.

Watching Trevor Arklow lay all this out while making it sound commonplace, an unremarkable part of a job, was a masterclass in manipulation. I learned just as much about wordplay that day as I learned about Collision, and when the meeting was over I left the room utterly committed to the opportunity I had been offered. Archie was right. I did need to thank her. Part of me will always be grateful. A small part. The part that isn't damaged beyond repair.

Training began.

In my world there is a thing called a training montage. It's a series of images that condenses many hours, days, weeks, months of hard work into a minute that hints at the struggle, then focuses on the result, as if the gains are a foregone conclusion. It makes us all blind as to the difficulty of achievement, and the pain that necessitates real growth. We all believe, deep down, that we would be geniuses were we but given the opportunity. It's only circumstance that stands in our way—or, more accurately, other people. Other people are always the problem, in our eyes, maiming our perfection.

If I was to sum up the next three months as a training montage I would show you:

Moments of reading, moments of waiting, moments of intense conversation and furrowed frowns, as Arklow taps on his keyboard and the whiteboard bears complex symbols.

I would show you:

The four of us in tracksuits, running on the flight deck of the *Iris*, the bone-grey sea of the Solent behind us, the rain plastering our hair to our heads, indistinguishable from our sweat. Star jumps, press-ups, burpees. We stand a little straighter, we suck in our stomachs. Our complexions improve. *Train the body, and you train the mind*, says Trevor Arklow.

I would show you:

Each of us practising our specialisation, over and over.

Gwen Last was the only one of us who instantly looked at home in the outfit of the other world, in flowing natural trousers and a loose shirt. She did not look as if she was auditioning for some bit part in a historical drama, and I could see how part of her talent was to be unnoticeable. People would forget her presence, and speak freely. She would blend in, disappear, and she had the most prodigious memory

I had ever come across. Trevor set her a daily routine. She memorised a number of small items, placed on a plastic tray from the cafeteria: a watch, a pebble, a cheap toy, a piece of fruit, on and on, and he added to it, took away from it, it made no difference. She recalled them all. Or Trevor would make long speeches, or recite pages from dusty old tomes, bringing archaic characters with strange names into the training suite, and she would repeat them all back. I was amazed by her, and yet the talent seemed separate from the woman. I could not say whenever she entered or left a room, and I could find nothing to say to her.

Perhaps this was not helped by the presence of Archie, who practised the art of being the centre of attention like it was a career, which I suppose it was. Or perhaps it would be closer to the truth to say it represented, for her, a possibility of escape from whatever she had been. I believe escape can be the sole goal of a life.

Every day Trevor sent her to a different level of the *Iris* to charm someone new. Employee, visitor, it did not matter. She was tasked with returning with some piece of information that should have been impossible to retrieve from a stranger, such as a mother's maiden name, or the name of a first pet. She never failed. I wouldn't say she grew in confidence as she practised, for she already seemed full of her own self-worth (necessary for her talent, I suppose), but as the weeks went past she grew into the clothes we tried on, veering towards the richer outfits of the wealthier classes in that world, who occasionally frequented the market. I think she was creating her own backstory, even then.

Alex Tee was a good soul. His skill with a pen was as fast as his speech. He could capture a likeness in seconds, and what's more, he could do it in any style: a caricature, a soft impressionistic likeness, or even photographic quality. Nothing was beyond him when it came to drawing. It was as if he lived on a faster speed than the rest of us, and yet there was something profoundly insular about him. He didn't make eye contact or look for conversation beyond formality. I liked him very much, found him restful, and stood near him at coffee breaks, chatting about the weather. We moaned about the state of the world. I didn't enjoy the feeling Gwen gave me, in contrast—as if every detail of me was being recorded for later regurgitation.

Meanwhile, I practised my magic.

Trevor had the idea of signing me up for a course on circus skills, and I went along willingly to one of the forts that lay along the ridgeline above Portsmouth, committing to a regular class where we tackled knife-throwing, juggling, riding a unicycle, tightrope walking. That took up Mondays and Tuesdays, and for the rest of the working week I would make objects appear and disappear for hours. My co-workers had a limited patience for this, so I began to tell stories as I practised, hoping to both keep and misdirect their attention.

The stories grew wilder, more fanciful, over time. I made them up as I went along, and loved the moments when I could see my mark stop looking at my hands and concentrate only on my words.

Archie was not so easily distracted. She only had to see me approach her with a deck of cards, and she would flutter her eyes, and say, "If you must practise upon me, sir, then I must practise upon you." She would deign to be amused and delighted by whatever trick I performed and tale I told, as if it was the first time she had ever witnessed such an act, and I would try hard not to be sucked into her charm. I can't explain it. It was always a battle to be separate from her desires, her plans. I did not want to simply become another pawn in her long game, and I would not have her claim me.

At the end of three months of training we were a team, of sorts. Strangely skilled, oddly conjoined.

Trevor Arklow called us together at the end of a Friday, looked us over, and said, "You're ready."

The job was simple: manipulate events through the collision to create a situation upon which people could bet. The situation, and therefore the odds, could be determined in advance, giving more control to Collision while also giving more excitement to the punters. Interest had begun to dry up. There were only so many times one could bet upon how many fruits a certain person would choose, even if that person was in another world.

Gwen was sent in very early the next day. We accompanied her down to the long expanse of the hangar bay, to see the real collider for the first time.

It was not bright, or colourful. There was no visible marketplace on the other side. The vast metal space of the hangar, three decks high, was filled with machinery, and there was a strong feeling of charge in the air—the kind that makes the hairs on your body stand to attention. Within the humming and the vast gadgetry was a ring of steel, small, that would have been easy to overlook. A nest of cables snaked up to it, along the floor, and disappeared inside.

At its centre was—nothing. Darkness. A hole, except the more I looked into it, the more it seemed *full* to me: the contents dry, grainy, like sand. I had the sudden belief that if the machines were all turned off as one, the sand, or maybe dust, would spill on to the floor, and that would be the end of the world beyond.

I preferred the story to the reality—a portal that led directly to the busy market. I suspect part of me had always been a disbeliever, but only at that moment did I see there might have been an advantage in believing. It was better to think of a welcoming, happy world, and an easy path to understand it. This dark sand, that had to be pushed through—wouldn't it feel like a violation to enter a place in such a way? Yes, it was a violation. But it changed nothing. I had been trained to do a job. I was a trickster, and there was nobody left on this planet who would be fooled.

A cordon of yellow tape, the long ends hanging messily down, had been set around the circle. Gwen and Trevor approached. Gwen was in her market outfit: not rich, not poor. Trevor lifted the tape and she ducked her head, and moved before the hole. I could hear nothing but the humming. Archie was beside me. She reached out, clutched my shirt front. Alex, on the other side of me, took a step back.

Gwen put out her hands, crouched. It was such a small hole. She knelt and leaned into it, made contact with the sand—I thought I saw it run over her fingers, her wrists, up to her arms—and she overbalanced, toppled in, was swallowed. Was gone. Archie swore.

Trevor came back to us, and shouted over the hum, "That was normal. That was normal." He looked sweaty. We followed him up to the suite and interrupted the cleaners, hard at work on the detritus of last night's gamblers. The chairs and sofas were in disarray, used glasses everywhere, and the smell of booze thick, every surface tacky with it. The view of the collider was black, and I felt fear for Gwen, for us all, as if that black would claim us. But the others did not express fear. Neither did I. I clung to Trevor's words. This was somehow normal. I ignored my thoughts, my feelings. *This is normal*, I said to myself.

Trevor asked the cleaners to come back later, and we had the suite to ourselves.

"There's usually a ten-minute delay," he said, "but I've asked them to make it a live feed for this." He checked his watch. "Now."

He was right. The collider, obviously a screen, flickered to life, and the market was revealed. It was early morning there, too. I had never thought about it before—the strangeness of that parallel timing. All was still, the stalls covered in woven blankets, the patterns only just visible in the beginning of the day. A group of small birds, in a cluster, hopped across the dirt road, scuffling at scraps dropped from the day before.

"It should take her seven minutes to get from the entry point to the market," Trevor said. "Sit." So we sat. Archie and Alex took the sofa reserved for high rollers, directly in front of the screen, and I chose an armchair further back, leaving the view at an angle. There was something about it I did not want to face head on. Trevor fetched us all gins. It was very good quality, fragrant and barely oily on the tongue, served to us in hefty crystal tumblers. I sipped mine. It was far too early to drink, wasn't it? Archie knocked hers back and held out the glass for more.

I've known long minutes in my life, but that was beyond an age. The little birds took off, as one.

Gwen entered slowly, crept into the view of the camera, her back to us. She looked suspicious. I had thought she'd looked so comfortable in her clothes, but instantly she was a ridiculous, incongruous sight, to my eyes at least. She reminded me of a pantomime villain, and I thought:

The pantomime villain enters the stage, creeps on tiptoe, back hunched, fingers flexed, mischief on her mind, and the crowd goes boo, *boo to you and your bad intentions, boo to you and the broken intentions you bear—*

"Good," said Trevor.

I heard relief in his voice. For all his reassurances, he had not been certain she would make it.

Gwen took small steps down the street.

I'd seen punters glued to the tiniest event. It was our turn. Archie said something to Alex. I didn't catch it. Alex did not reply. I looked at Archie's glass. It was empty again. I put down my own, unfinished. Alex's was untouched. I looked over my shoulder, at Trevor, as tall and straight as ever. Why didn't I want to look at the screen? I could not bear to look at the screen.

"There," breathed Trevor.

I had to look.

Gwen was doubled over. She straightened. She moved back, without turning, step by step, gradual. It took a long time for her body to move out of sight of the camera.

She had left an object on the ground. It was a small cube. Small enough to fit easily in the palm.

I felt it, then: the pull of the game. I wanted to know. It was a cube, maybe only a cube, maybe nothing more. Unimportant. It did not matter. It was a possibility that nobody would even spot it, that they might kick it under one of the stalls. They might step over it. They might gather around it, wonder what it was, how it was made. Was it hand-crafted, to fit with what

186

we thought we knew about that world, or was it some mass-produced, glued wood-substitute that would confound them? Would one person take it up, selfishly hoard it, cherish it? I wanted to know. I wanted to know.

The door clicked. I looked around. Trevor was gone. Perhaps he was on the way to meet Gwen, greet her as she emerged. On the screen, nothing happened. We watched and watched as daylight came further towards the market, creeping down over the bricks of the surrounding buildings to reach the canopies of the stalls, then bring bright colours back to the woollen blankets. I distrusted it all intensely at that moment. It couldn't be real. This was part of the game, the game played by Archie, by Trevor, by Collision. Archie was clenching her jaw, holding her once-more-empty glass too tightly. We did not speak.

When Gwen and Trevor came through the door of the suite together, I saw how they had formed a connection through the experience. Trevor had been on the other side of the collision too, at some point, I was certain of it. Gwen perched at the back of the room, on one of the bar stools. The mirror, above her, held the secret of our training area. She said, "Have they found it yet?" Her voice was loud, sharp-edged. She had never spoken in such a way before.

"Not yet," said Alex, and we all waited some more, waited until it seemed ridiculous that somebody had not started their day, arrived at the market bearing goods to be sold. There were sounds from further down the corridor, then a knock on the door. Trevor answered it—the cleaners, wanting to be admitted. He sent them away again, the conversation tense.

Nobody came to the market.

I thought: *we've broken it.*

No.

No, it began to wake. Someone arrived, one of the regular stallholders, the one who was always among the first, a conscientious salesman. I recognised him. Others followed. They shook out their blankets, folded them, slipped them under the stalls. They began the business of laying out their produce, brought in heavy bags and boxes. It was too early for much custom, and they smiled and chatted between themselves. Then the shift in intention as the first customers came, and the smiles of the traders turned outwards in the hope of a sale.

Nobody saw the cube.

I thought: *It's invisible to them, things from here can't be seen there,* and I was glad. I almost spoke it aloud. I had to hold it back. But all delusions end, and the one who saw it, stooped for it, scooped it up, was a little girl who couldn't have been more than a few years old.

She let go of her father's hand and reached for it. He was distracted, looking at the vegetables on the closest stall. He let her go easily. In my world it would be enough to be labelled as a bad parent, but what was there for them to be afraid of? There was no threat but what we had created. The cube. It was a threat, somehow. She picked it up, turned it in her hands.

She faced the camera perfectly but she couldn't have known that. Like a script. People walked close by, in front of the lens, blocking our view, and for one ridiculous moment I craned my neck to attempt to see around them. "Move!" Archie said, and as they parted we focused once more on the tiny hands, the cube. Her father came back to her, knelt, and she gave the cube to him. They looked at it together. His fingers turned it over, hesitated. They found a catch somewhere. The cube unlocked, unfolded rather, to a flat shape, the pieces interlocked. There was something inside, small and white.

The father took it up. It was a rectangle. A piece of card, maybe. Someone stepped in front of the lens once more and we all groaned.

"For fuck's sake!" said Archie.

The man in front of the lens moved on, and the father and daughter moved to the stall closest to them, to the right of the screen—one that sold jewellery, with many necklaces hanging from pegs mounted along the supports and crossbeams. The woman who ran it always wore her long hair up, wrapped around the crown of her head, to reveal dangling earrings, shaped like bells. The father handed the white slip to her, and she looked at it closely, then leaned forward, and spoke. He shook his head.

On the right, the stallholder took down a necklace from a peg and handed it to the father, who gave it to the daughter. Her delight permeated the lens, soaked through the screen. We all bathed in it. The father placed it around her neck, helped her with the clasp. The stallholder kept the slip and the unfolded box, and slid them under the stall.

We watched as the father and daughter, if that was what they were, concluded their shopping and wandered out of view. New customers came forward.

I couldn't sit down. I wanted to reach through the screen, to get my answers.

"What happened?" said Alex. "What just happened?"

"It was a note," said Trevor. He still stood by the bar. He hadn't moved. Gwen was beside him. She had looked out of place in the other world, and now she looked incongruous in this one: her face, somehow simpler, her expression soft. It did not suit the gambling suite of the rich and mighty, with the smell of them still in the air.

"A note," Archie said, her voice sharp, wondering.

"A gift."

"What kind of gift?"

"No, no." Trevor cleared his throat. "That's what the note said. *A gift for you.*"

"In their language?" I asked. "You know their language?"

"It's the same," he said.

"Our languages are the same," Trevor repeated, and Archie laughed, and said, "A gift for you."

A knock on the door, this time no excuses. The room had to be cleaned, and we returned to our secret place behind the mirror. I left my gin by the side of the armchair, tucked by the front leg.

I think I have never been a stupid man. I knew it made no sense. I could see that clearly. How could two separate worlds have developed the same language? What were the ramifications of that within so many scientific fields? I couldn't comprehend it. I thought of the cube that had sprung apart, and could not be reassembled. My construction of this world, how it slotted together and how it existed, was in pieces. The people, the customs, the jolly comings and goings of the market, the peaceful society, the idealised quality of everything down to the light that shone from their sky: it all looked like it had been imagined by some class-conscious university professor from Oxford in the 1930s. It could not be real. It could not possibly be real.

All day long, in the training room, I practised my tricks. I didn't speak. I didn't know how to voice my thoughts.

The world had to be real.

I'd seen Gwen in there. I'd watched her push through the black sand, and she had emerged changed by her experience. Didn't that define reality? I watched her, and the others, and I practised all day. I had too many questions to begin to ask them, and I was afraid of what I might lose if I did. I had already begun the process of transformation, and I did not want it to end.

As we wrapped up that day, Trevor asked me to stay behind.

We faced each other, at either end of the long table. Through the window, the usual gamblers were being served, and the market was packing up. It seemed obvious a new level of excitement needed to be added to keep the money rolling in. This was an escalating game.

"I know," Trevor said, "the chances of having a shared language are astronomically slight. Beyond that, it has implications. It's being investigated by people very much more intelligent than us. By experts. But that's why we need a constant revenue stream. So that study can continue into what this all means. The origins of language, the way that societies form, the kinds of interactions that leads to, the theological impact…"

"It's huge, isn't it?" I said. "I can't even begin to…" I wanted to say: *Send me to these experts. Better still, make me an expert. Sponsor me through university, and give me the tools I need to make sense of this.*

"Me neither."

"Archie said—" I stopped, feeling disloyal.

"She told you nobody is studying the collider. She tries to tie people to her by saying whatever she thinks will cut their bonds to other people, other institutions. She wants you to be reliant on her alone. You know to take it all as part of her charm, I think. I've seen you sizing her up, refusing to play by her rules. Look, I've been thinking about it. You should be next through to the market. You can see it all for yourself. Does that work for you? Leave your questions, your doubts, on this side. Over there you can be the master of your own destiny, if that's what you want. You can be anything at all. It's a wonderful feeling."

"You've been there," I said.

"I was one of the first through. I took samples, made first contact. Set up the camera, the equipment. It helps if you accept you're not the same there. Compartmentalise. Have a different name, a different personality. Think about it. Tell me what you want to do by morning."

I said goodbye, determined to think it over, but the truth was that it didn't even take the distance of the ferry ride back to my car to know—I was no longer simply Miles Green. I needed a name that represented the new person that gestated inside me, and now had to be born.

I decided on the name: Marius Mondegreen.

Two days later I took my first push through the black sand.

It did not feel as it looked. It did not have a texture, a coarseness. It was only a moment, cool and smooth on the skin, a slight change in resistance, like walking through a breeze, and yet I felt I emerged with a clarity to me, a cleanliness. Perhaps it was only the worry of the journey that had been removed, but it felt greater than that to me. Some alterations are profound before we have time to process their meaning. Not so the return journey to the *Iris*, at the end of my first shift as Mondegreen. I felt something weighty, doughy, sink inside me, and settle back into place.

I won't go into drawn-out detail about every mission I then undertook.

I will say that when I was on missions, planting an item or manufacturing an event, I felt utterly integrated, and I think that translated to the screen, too, somehow penetrating the lens of the camera to reach those who were betting on the outcome. My team-mates felt it too. Once, over coffee, Alex asked me, "How do you do it?"

"What?" I said.

"*Belong* like you do."

By that point we had both been on regular missions. I had seen him at work, sketching people and leaving the likenesses for them to find. He blended in beautifully to the world, I thought. "You belong too," I told him.

"Not like you. I'm a nobody there. You—you look like you were born important."

I thought about that often. I liked it more than I can say.

The games were popular, and for a while it was enough. Small variations were added. Innocent intentions became murkier, over time. I used sleight of hand to steal an object from one stall and put it on another, triggering an argument. Alex drew strange symbols in chalk on the wooden beams of a crockery stall, and the holder barely looked at them before scrubbing them off with a cloth. Archie browsed like an empress and haggled like a merchant, the goal being to get an item, any item at all, for free. She managed it more often than not. Then she turned to seducing locals, seeing if she could persuade them into action for her. Would they take off their shoes? Or tell her a piece of highly personal information? The gamblers watched, avid. I wondered if they, too, felt the pull of that world.

The *Iris*, Portsmouth, the news, the whole sorry mess of society, faded in colour and texture for me. Only the other world was vivid. My birth name no longer felt comfortable. The games were escalating, and it was not sustainable. One of my names had to end. I knew it. And I lived for those moments in the market. So many people did, gamblers and workers alike.

Then Gwen went in and did not come back.

At first, nobody paid much attention. She was late back. That was all. Time stretched out. Later. Later. The day wore on. We waited in the room behind the suite. The game she had been sent across to set up could not be played, and the punters who had already placed their bets moaned, a little. Their bets were refunded, and after all, there would always be a new game tomorrow. It was mid-afternoon when Trevor mentioned Gwen would certainly be back before the end of the working day because of her husband and daughter. So strange, to think of her tied to this place. She had never once mentioned them to me.

Five o'clock came and went. Trevor sighed and said he would inform Collision management. He seemed resigned to the loss of her, as if it was all out of his hands.

"What if she's hurt?" I said.

"It's not that," said Archie, and I knew what she was thinking, what we were all thinking. We were only surprised that she was the first to run away.

"It's a good point," said Trevor, as if Archie hadn't spoken. "Does somebody want to go through and check?"

I volunteered. How precarious it all suddenly felt: that one small portal, and the good grace or the blind eye of the systems of my world, allowing me to come and go. Gwen's disappearance jeopardised that.

Through the portal, on the other side of the black sand, was a large cellar built in the same red brick as the market houses. It was dimly lit by solar lamps that were replaced by one of us every day, taken out and left on the deck of the *Iris* to recharge. Crates were stacked high under the arches of that underground space—unlabelled wooden boxes, that could have belonged to either world. But I had checked the contents of one with curiosity on a previous visit, and found it filled with tools and electrical equipment, and the smooth, cold, shaped metals of my technology-addicted world. Strange, how they could be familiar and unidentifiable to me at the same time. I was no electrician.

A flight of wooden steps led up to a trapdoor in the ceiling that rose to allow access to a tiny dark space, like standing inside a wardrobe, and from there, a door opened on to a quiet back alley, one turn away from the market. It was dusk.

I expected—I don't know—some obvious and immediate sign of Gwen. A note on a crate, maybe, or a pile of clothes. Something. The signs of a suicide, it occurs to me now. Wasn't it a form of death, to choose to leave an entire world behind? When there was nothing of Gwen's waiting for me, I thought for a moment: *She's been kidnapped. Murdered.* Then I pushed such thoughts away. *Things like that don't happen here*, I told myself. Was that naïve?

I made my way to the market, and looked at the last stragglers, the packing up, the fading of the light. I was aware of the camera at my back, high up, worked into the brick. The smell of the sea was strong, from the used crates of the eel sellers, a local delicacy.

The wine merchant, who stayed open a little later most days, recognised me and held out a taster glass with a smile. I took it, and we exchanged a few words. His name was Gregon, I remember. A large, hearty man with a beard to be admired. No doubt he later died in the destruction of Droad, but at that moment he was there, and warm-hearted, and keen to discuss this particularly good wine that had come from grapes grown on the lower slopes of the hills in the east. He told me he had family there, via marriage—a brother-in-law. Gregon, good with wine. I sipped it. It was too sweet for my tastes. One to pair with a dessert, maybe.

Gregon said, "You've missed the crowds. Another good day."

"I'm late, I know. Are you packing up?"

He nodded. "Reaching the end of the Venerabild," he said, or something like it, "and we'll be changing to Udocta." Seasons? Place names? Something to do with the wine trade, perhaps. I've never found out. He made a face as if I was expected to respond, so I did, pulling an expression that sat between expressions. Then I produced a boiled sweet from thin air and handed it to him. Everyone over there was crazy about them: the sugar, the instant hit of it, the bright colours. I always carried them.

"You'll have to tell me how these are made," he said, then popped it into his mouth.

"Family secret," I said, and winked. I knew he understood that. I asked, then, after Gwen: *Have you seen...? Older relative, given to wandering...?* That sort of thing.

"I think I know who you mean," he said, "Seen her around. She didn't look local. I wondered if she was one of the visitors that have been coming for the oddness."

"The oddness?" I said. The way he said it suggested it was a new concept for him, too. I held the delicate taster glass by its long stem, between my thumb and forefinger.

"That's what we're calling it. The things happening around here in the past months. It's not an old energy, not like you get at the low seas. Strange things happen, but small things. Little boxes, and marks on the stalls and the walls, and drawings. There's a tingling in the air, too. Can't you feel it?"

I made a movement with my head that might have been a nod. "So the market is busier now?" I asked. "I'm new to the area. I've got nothing to compare it with."

"Word got around," Gregon said. "People started to come. To feel it, maybe to have an oddness happen to them. And round the corner"—he pointed down the street, to where the camera could not see—"the calculators set up stall. People wager on what might happen on a particular day. Well, the world has always been that way, but I must admit I preferred the market before it became a place upon which to wager. You really have not been to Droad before? Where are you from?"

"I go where the world takes me," I said, "and I do not ask the wind to explain itself. That would be a waste of everyone's breath."

"Hah."

I finished my glass, returned it to Gregon, and made my way back to the basement.

When I returned to the training room, I told Trevor and the others that Gwen was gone for good.

That night I did not return to my parents' house. I went to a pub on the seafront, stared at the row of optics for a while, thinking of how much I preferred the blown glass of the other world. I wasn't drunk when I decided to go to Archie's flat; I was only in that meditative state that two or three pints can bring. I felt the intensity of the moment. *Now or never,* that was what I said to myself, over and over.

When I rang her doorbell, she buzzed me up to her flat as if we had made a longstanding agreement to meet and I was running a few minutes late. "At last," she said, waiting in the doorway for me. She ushered me in, to the main room, where the couch and the rolltop desk stood in place. An elderly man and woman stood there, both in well-cut business suits. The man had his back to me, looking out of the window. The woman had obviously just stood up from the couch, and was hovering, looking uncomfortable.

"They're just leaving," Archie said.

"Yes," said the woman.

"This is Marius," Archie told them, using my other name.

"Hello," I said.

I saw a flash of recognition in the woman's eyes. She said, "Lovely."

"These are my parents," Archie said, in a voice so tart, so gleeful, that it was obvious she'd lied, and wanted me to see it. The woman stared at her. The man did not turn around. "Right then, off you go."

"Goodbye," said the woman. "Lovely to meet you. Lovely." She was retreating further and further into her own Englishness—a well-worn defence mechanism, no doubt. She walked past me, keeping as much distance as she could, and the man followed her. His profile was familiar: the sideburns were long, well-shaped, and the skin of his cheek was very smooth and shiny. I couldn't place him.

Archie shut the door behind them, then crossed to the window and looked out. "Just making sure," she said.

"That they're going? Strange, to be so suspicious of your own parents."

"Is it?"

I thought of my own, at home, watching television. "Who are they, really?" I asked her, but I knew she wouldn't answer. Instead she offered me coffee, and I accepted, and it was a strange echo of that morning months ago, when I had wanted so badly to impress her, except this time I knew all we were doing was biding time until she got to the point of saying what she wanted.

It took about a quarter of a cup. I sat on the sofa, and she prowled the flat, still glancing out of the window every now and again.

"Gwen's timing sucks," she said. "Trevor can't hush it up for long. There'll be a crackdown. These kind of events—they change things. Make it so things can't be moved. Do you know what I mean?"

I thought she was patronising me. I said, "Are you going to make the leap or not?" That was it. That was the question I had come here to ask.

She drew down the blind, and it made the room feel smaller, airless. "I wanted to ask you the same thing, Marius."

"In that case, I thank you for your consideration."

She curtseyed. It introduced a note of wary formality that, I think, suited us both. "Either we go together," she said, "or it doesn't happen."

"I agree."

"And it has to be tomorrow, or it doesn't happen."

"Absolutely."

She came to me, took my coffee cup, put it down on the grubby carpet that had seen better days. She knelt before me so our eyes were level. Her woollen grey dress would have looked equally at home in the other world, I realised. She was already halfway there, in her head. She held my gaze.

The way people look, the way they wear their hair, their clothes, their attitudes: over time, all this fades into the background, and you can begin to see the performative nature of living, and how, beneath that, there's a core of existence. It's the piece of grit around which the elaborate armour of personality forms. At that moment I got my first glimpse of the grit of her, and I feared her.

But I could not give up being Marius, or stifle him under terms and conditions. I could not cut myself in two and discard the greater part.

"Get there early tomorrow," she said. "I'm down for the game anyway, and lamp replacement. You can say you're helping. We'll both just walk through."

"Nobody has needed help before."

"Nobody's made a note of who's coming and going before, and I think we'll have another day before Collision starts paying attention, or Gwen's family makes enough fuss. Do you know why I recommended you for this job?"

"Does it matter? The person you recommended is on the way out. Nearly gone. Forget it." I meant it, absolutely. If this was to work, she had to see me as an equal. I didn't know if she was capable of that.

"Of course," she said. She bowed her head. Mock submission. She crawled forwards and climbed on to the sofa beside me. She did not touch me, but I felt her spiky attempt to be companionable. She was tolerating me, perhaps even liked to be close. "I will try," she said. "I'm changing too, you know? I'll change again. We don't know how to live over there, not really. We know one basement, one door, one street. How do we cope?"

"We'll weave our ignorance into our stories. Make it part of our charm."

"Always the stories, with you." She considered then said, "Besides, if you can survive this city, you can survive anything, right? And we'll have each other." She winked at me. I smiled, a little, to show I appreciated the indulgence without believing in it. She put out her hand, and I took it, and we sat there, together, for a while. It wasn't much of a plan, but we were betting that it didn't need to be, as long as we moved fast.

The next morning, we met outside the collider room. We were both dressed as the people we wanted to be. I wore my loose trousers and white shirt, with a warm cape and hard boots. I had secreted as many of my accessories as I could about my person, mindful that once I ran out of boiled sweets there would be no more. Archie wore her long grey dress with her hair up, strands criss-crossing the crown of her head. Around her shoulders was a white fleecy blanket, the one that had been draped over her ageing sofa, and she wore it as if it was an expensive fur. We both had the standard leather satchels provided by Collision slung on our backs. I did not ask what she had deemed necessary to pack within hers, and she did not inquire about mine.

It seemed she was correct: No measures had been put in place yet. All was quiet. The usual guard by the door did not even spare us a second glance. It was only as we entered the collider room and found Trevor Arklow standing there, between us and the portal, that I realised the gamble could never have paid off. He'd had the measure of us all along.

His arms crossed over his chest and his feet planted firmly apart, like a schoolteacher dominating a classroom, he said, "I hate to be proven right, sometimes." The cordon was behind him, the orange tape in place. His positioning, his words, felt as planned and inevitable as his training timetable; it had always been heading to this moment.

We walked towards him, Archie and I, our steps in synchronicity. We stopped a few metres away.

"Bit melodramatic for you, Trevor," she said.

"I wouldn't have opted for a showdown, given the chance. But you didn't, did you? Give me the chance to have it otherwise. This is more to your taste than mine."

"This is all still according to the plan."

"Whose plan?" Trevor pointed at me. "Does Miles know?"

"He's his own man," she said. "He doesn't need to be dragged into this."

Trevor uncrossed his arms, scratched the back of his neck. "I'm not going to bother to refute that."

"Somebody has to find Gwen and bring her back," I said.

"Is that what you think you're doing?" Trevor said, but his attention remained on Archie, and I could understand why. How weak I must have looked to him, then, obeying commands and believing what I was told. *He underestimates me,* I told myself. It was to my advantage. Better to look weak, toothless, and present no threat. If his attention was on Archie, I had time to size up the situation. I looked around me; there was nobody in the shadows, no reinforcements. As far as I could see, he hadn't brought help. Perhaps that meant he was operating outside the remit of Collision, working to his own agenda. One he thought he shared with Archie.

"Nothing has changed," she said, slowly, clearly. "You'll have to trust me on that."

"Is Gwen part of it too?"

"I'm as surprised as you are by Gwen. That's why we're having to move quickly. We'll go across now, find her. Bring her back. You smooth things over here. Tell everyone it's all on track."

"They're never going to buy that with three of you gone."

"Long-term operations," she said. "It's always been what they're after."

"Gwen has a family," Trevor snapped.

Archie shrugged. The fleece shifted on her shoulders, and she moved it back into position, high up, around her neck. "That's the kind of problem you're good at solving, isn't it?"

"The husband has called the police."

"So what?"

"The police will speak to Collision."

"You'll think of something," she said.

"No, *you'll* think of something, Alice," he said. "And until you do, nobody goes through. You sold it, you deliver it."

"Trevor—"

"Nobody." He made a show of checking his watch. "I've been here all night waiting for you to show up. There's enough time for a coffee before we start trying to sort this mess out. Get changed, and I'll shout you both breakfast. We've got a busy planning day ahead."

She said, "Well, fine then, but it would have been much easier if you just let us go and look for her properly." She took steps backwards, not turning around. "She can't have got far, she's probably still in Droad, we had an idea to look in a radial pattern, the two of us have connections in the city now. It would be much better to simply bring her back—"

"Who's to say you'll be able to persuade her to return?" Trevor asked. He took two steps forward, away from the cordon, to draw level with me.

It was easy. He was not a strong man, tall and sinewy but very light, as if he barely ate—where was his pleasure in life? He was a man of business. He thought basic rules of behaviour applied. I ran at him, let momentum take me; I hit him around the knees and he fell to the floor. Archie was ready. I swear she enjoyed jumping over him, clearing the cordon, her skirt belling out. I followed her and we dived into the black sand headfirst, feeling the cold, clean sweep of the portal to the cellar of the world beyond.

"Quick, quick," she called, and we kept running, took the stairs two at a time, burst through the door beyond. At the side street she turned left instead of right, away from the market, and she slowed her pace and reached for me, took my hand in hers. Her grip was strong, and her fingernails bit into my palm, but I did not try to pull away. I was hers. The paved street widened, and a few people were walking, mainly delivering bread, milk, fruits in the baskets and carts they all used. We reached a bend in the street and found ourselves in an open space—a plaza, dotted with cultivated small trees, red brick buildings rising around us, and there was a low wall at the far end. We crossed to it, leaned over it. Beneath us was a strong, flowing river pouring into the sea, sparkling in the early morning sun, with the small circular boats of the fishermen upon it. There were so many of them, with their nets suspended from the short central masts, lowered then raised to reveal slithering bounties—eels. The view was alive with them. Every net lowered was retrieved filled to capacity, so plenteous that the entire city could have been fed twice over, it seemed to me—no guilt, no shame, no thought of whether the same amount would be available tomorrow, or what would happen in the weeks and months to come. No sense of individual responsibility regarding overfishing or exploitation, no sense of being outside of the natural order of that world. No expectation of reassurance needed by whomever put that eel in their mouth. No end to the coast, its gifts, no delineation between river and city.

I let go of Archie's hand.

We stood in silence, for a time.

I understood, then, that I could not become part of this world if I had to look her in the eyes, every day, and see everything I hated about the world I had left behind.

Eventually she said, "If you're going, I won't ever think ill of you for it. All plans must change. We never agreed to be together no matter what."

"All plans change," I agreed. "Even long-term ones."

She stood very still, then licked her lips and said, "I never meant to go through with it."

"Bigger stories. Bigger bets. What was it to be?"

"This place isn't—It has a history. Trevor found a library. There were books about the problems it's had in the past. Issues that led to conflicts. It's been at war for hundreds of years."

"War."

"A cold war. Trevor saw an opportunity to use… fault lines that can be manipulated to create large-scale stories, with conclusions that can be calculated."

"Trevor came up with this alone?"

She shook her head.

It came to me: at her flat, the woman and the man. The man had refused to look directly at me. I had known him. One of the high rollers, in the suite. "A—what do you call it? A consortium? A manipulation? I don't know the collective noun for gamblers hoping to play the system."

"A boredom," she said, with a smile, a wince.

"You both worked for them. Otter Enterprises."

She lifted her chin. "I told you—I never intended to go through with it. Trevor approached me, introduced me to his backers, and I didn't look unwilling. The longer they believed in me, the longer I could stall them, have time to find other solutions. Marius—"

"What?"

Over the river, over the skyline of the city, the quality of light was changing, awakening, to become the bright blue of a busy summer day. "We are similar, aren't we? In ways I don't want to analyse, to break down into the words we've been given to describe such emotions. In terms of buyer and seller, not give and take. Because of that similarity, I find I don't want you to think ill of me."

I nodded. I leaned forward, against the wall. The fishermen, so attuned to the light and its meaning, were bringing in their catches. Their work was over for the day. I had to pull a great disappearing act. Still, I couldn't move. Not quite yet.

"I am a person who has had to make opportunities," she said, "then grasp them tightly. Such a life doesn't suit a moral approach."

"Maybe it didn't, back where we started. But I feel it might, here."

"Redemption?" She snorted, but I could tell the word appealed to her.

"Perhaps you should try it."

"Where will you go?"

"It's a blank map. Any road will lead to my destination."

"How do you do it?" she said, turning to face me. "How do you sound so perfect for this place?"

"It has seeped into me."

"Yes. That's it. It has already shaped us, hasn't it? And it will shape us further."

"The war," I said. "The war you planned to start."

"Don't."

"They won't give up on it. A cold war is such a different beast from a hot one. It will do terrible things to this world."

"Maybe Gwen's disappearance, our disappearance, will be enough. The government will get involved. Start paying attention to what's happening. Regulate the collider."

I knew she couldn't possibly believe that, but I understood her desire to live only in the moment, *for* the moment, and to leave behind responsibility. And who could blame her? It was such a beautifully fresh start, and she looked a vision, with her fake fur over her shoulders and her eyes very clear.

"Well," I said, "We can run, simply for the joy of it, for a while."

"Let's do that." She moved into my arms. I held her, my neck against the fur, watching the last of the boats get pulled to shore. Then I walked away.

I didn't see her again for an age.

I heard about her, at parties and gatherings, anywhere the rich and powerful gathered and invited me along to make their entertainment: I heard the talk of the survivor of the mountains, the far-north friend of an allynx, wearing a fur so soft that it had to be touched to be believed: the human raised wild, curled up in a cave against the legendary big cat. And she had scoffed at my predilection for stories. I was told of how she was having to relearn the niceties of society, but was utterly charming in her naivety and wonder. I turned down events where she might appear, didn't travel far north.

Then I overheard the news: she was to be made a Syld. She had found favour with the ruling families of the north. It was not a position that had an equivalent in the old world, and nobody offered any real explanation of it. It's still one of the hazy spots in my understanding. What is a Syld? Not elected, not acquired by money or position. An agreement was needed but the reasoning never made public, and nobody ever questioned it. Does the key to happiness lie in this form of agreement, reached without words, or is that a symptom of the unbroken society?

I thought about it long and hard; I craved the academic approach, the dismantling of what made the world work. The more tricks I pulled, the less I admired myself, and the news that Archie had achieved a level of integration beyond me was painful. They couldn't see the threat she represented. None of them could see it.

Over the years of thinking and performing, travelling and growing, I thought perhaps I had been forgotten. I cautiously returned to Droad, performing at the Mutuality. I thought of it as my birthplace. I was idiotic, perhaps. But there always did have to be an element of chance, of risk. Of danger.

Then: Alex.

I spotted him from my high wire, his face turned up to me. He had grown a beard, and that too was unrestrained and spiked, with a wired, electrical quality. He was trading in the square, outside the Mutuality, and he had his own stall among the many that were offering treats to the crowd for one of the many hatted festivals. They were my favourite events of the calendar, with a mingling of all sorts in good humour, free and easy and lasting until the first clouding over of the moon.

I froze on the wire, caught between the clock tower and the Mutuality balcony, but only for a moment. Alex's eyes were on me. He nodded. I felt the inevitability of it. Of course somebody would approach me, eventually. I had felt untouchable. It was good that it was a face I knew. I collected myself, I delivered a story to the crowd, accepted their applause. I conjured a bird to sing for them, perched on my finger, then let it fly free. As they watched it take to the air, a splash of red in the clear white sky, I slipped away, changed outfit, emerged from the Mutuality gates with my wide-brimmed hat pulled low, and made my way to the store where Alex was offering his drawings for sale.

Fantastical Visions

his card read, affixed to the front of the standard stall, and he sat on a stool behind the counter. Laid out were examples of his work. No more portraits, no more friendly faces in any style desired. These were intricate pen-and-ink pictures of events I recognised, machines I knew from the world that spawned us, and other, more imaginary flights. I saw skyscrapers on fire, vast explosions on islands, the sea peeling back from the crater like burnt skin. I saw guns and lasers and crowds bombarded by water cannons, cars and tanks. People fled, each face given a contorted expression. Tall towers at the ends of vast lakes, between the twin peaks of mountains.

"Hieronymus Bosch is such an inspiration," said Alex.

It was as if I had heard a foreign language, one I knew so well that I dreamt in it. I could not make sense of it now, but it could come back to me, I knew it, I would know it again: the names, the works of those who informed others. Yes, Bosch. It returned to me. I had seen a painting, once, in a gallery where I'd walked past one work after another, collected together in such a way that they become meaningless. White slips of paper underneath. Bodies, landscapes.

"Do people take any of these?" I asked him.

"Don't people always take what you give away? It's a festival. Freebies are part of the deal, right?"

"Where's the camera? What game are you playing?"

I looked him over. Had they found a way to connect him up, transmit a signal wirelessly across worlds? The thought made me feel sick.

"They stopped those sorts of games."

"Then you—you've come through on your own?"

He looked away, then down at his hands. He still held a pen: a... biro. Ingenious. He was halfway through a new drawing that I thought might be of a ship. Maybe even the *Iris*, with the Spinnaker in the background. "There's no such thing as being on your own," he said. "Everyone picked a side. You too."

"And you picked Collision?"

Browsers came to the stall, two young women, wearing their hats with broad brims pulled back, unlike my own. One glanced at me, but did not recognise me. Nobody ever did, if I was not attired in the style of Mondegreen. She looked back at the illustrations, and pointed to one of a city skyline I felt I should recognise. Airships floated above skyscrapers. One bloated ship bobbed above a sharp point, jutting from the highest building, to which it was tethered by the lightest stroke of the pen.

"What is it?" she said to Alex, full of curiosity.

"It's a drawing," he said, "Straight out of my mind," and she smiled, a confused but open return of his obvious humour.

"I would love to keep it," she said, shyly.

"Good deeds line the finest beds," he said, the traditional refrain, and he rolled it up and passed it to her. She took it with a quiet thank you. He took delight in the exchange, I could see it in the way he flourished it, presented it to her. I was reminded of the Alex I had once chatted with, beside the coffee machine, and our way of speaking to each other came back to me.

The women left, and I said, "What's it like back there, then?"

"Mate," he said, "It's a shitshow."

It was the perfect word. I laughed out loud.

"I can believe it."

"I'm serious," he said. "Consultants came in. They tell me what to draw and how to draw it. Apparently it's all about getting out certain messages."

"Like what?" Such a strange return to this use of language, like a deep dislocation that left no scratch on the surface. I felt odd, damaged.

"It's meant to stir a response."

I looked at the drawings again. What would others make of them, take away from them? It was impossible to tell. I couldn't see them with new eyes. Every part of them was informed by previous knowledge that remained locked within me. I never could be truly of this world, after all.

"We used to have a good old moan, didn't we? I wondered what I'd say if I saw you again," said Alex.

"Do you know now?"

He hesitated, nodded. "I want all this to stop, Miles. Help me find a way to make it stop."

I was the master tightrope walker. I had perfect balance, immaculate timing. "Tell me everything," I said, "and we will stop it."

We closed up his stall and took his illustrations to an inn I knew well on the outskirts of Droad. I kept a room there under another name; I had collected many names, by that point. The room was at the back of the always-busy building, on the top floor. I had bedecked the room in rich, warm colours, hanging cloaks from the posts of the bed and the knobs of the cupboard and wash stand, and I had a small window, the glass pane thicker at the bottom, just big enough for me to climb through. It was possible to move over the rooftops to the university, where I had cultivated other, more austere, connections.

It took a few minutes to get the fire in the small grate kindled, and we burned the drawings, making sure each was reduced to grey ash. It was satisfying, Alex said, although he cried during the process. He dashed away the tears with the back of his hand; I think he wished I hadn't seen them.

Then he paced the room, from window to door, sweating by the heat of the fire, and I sat on the bed and listened to the plans in place, as far as he knew. New trainees were coming, were weeks away from their first trips through the portal, and they would not reveal their specialities. Trevor did not train them; that was now the work of the consultants, and Trevor had a new role—he was coming and going from this world, involved in what he described as 'high-level negotiations' on both sides. He went to London, too, dealing with politicians and the public, who were becoming increasingly fractious at Collision's secrecy. Gwen's family had kicked up a stink, and the media had picked up hints of a good story. Attention had brought problems. Terrorist threats had been made.

I pictured Trevor working his way into power structures everywhere, trying to control the situation, with that quiet methodical approach he favoured, drilling little holes through things that had appeared solid to me. I thought, somehow, I would sense it if someone like him came through the portal and laid his eggs within. Ridiculous, I realised.

When Alex finished speaking, I passed him a handkerchief from one of my many inner pockets, and he wiped his face with it. He offered it back to me, and I refused it. Everything he touched felt like corruption. "So much has happened!" he said, but then failed to think of much to tell me beyond new names that had no meaning to me: people who had taken over the running of countries, of companies, or won sporting events. Everything was still urgent. Places were in drought, places were underwater. "There's a new sea defence system in Portsmouth!" he said, pleased to have remembered something that might act as a real connection, and then added that a new bakery had opened in Southsea that also did a decent flat white. A celebrity had died the week before, he said, and I thought of what a celebrity was, and how I might be described as one by people who could never understand how little that had to do with me, as a concept. Then I felt sick, sick at myself and at the way I was trying to exempt myself from such things even though they were still engrained in me.

Droad's identity had been revealed to me piecemeal over the years. It represented a cultural hive, a place of energetic conversation and co-operation. It had a style all of its own. Architecturally, artistically, it was fascinating in its detail, each building and public space a combination of north, south, old, new, but if you were not steeped in this world you would not see it. We left the inn and walked through its beauties. I pointed out all I could of why it was special, and in return Alex pointed out the new cameras in locations radiating out from the alley, concentrating in the area close to the Mutuality. We stood together outside that imposing building with its great dome, and the turrets and castellations that might look messy to the casual observer, and Alex said, "They've got access inside as well." How stupid, to think of their eyes still contained to the market, when I had known all along they had plans for expansion. They had seen me perform, then. I had never been beyond their reach, if they had cared to act. If they had thought me any threat to their plans, surely they would have acted.

We walked down to the bridge, by the mouth of the river. It was late afternoon, and the little boats of the many fishermen were stacked, high on the shoreline, with the masts removed and placed in a pile beside them, like kindling. The nets, too, folded. Two longer, lozenge-shaped boats were approaching from opposite sides. They passed each other, and those on the decks waved, or shouted greetings. Both boats were painted gold and green, striped diagonally: the colours of Droad.

Six years and a different life ago, I had leaned upon this wall with Archetta, and seen the same view with the eyes of an outsider who dreamed of integration. Was I different? Did I belong?

"Have you seen her?" I asked.

"Who?"

"Archie."

"You mean 'the grand Syld'?" He put on a posh voice, and I realised he had never liked her, much. It hadn't occurred to me that people could feel lukewarm towards her, when I was filled up by her, by our struggle against each other, for each other. "I was going to ask you the same thing."

"Or Gwen?"

He let out a long breath, his gaze on the approaching boat, and said, "People talk about you and Archie. The Allynx and the Misheard Word, right? And Trevor chose a name for himself too. He likes to be called the Oster. That's what they call otters over here, isn't it? But nobody mentions Gwen. Gwen never gets seen, anywhere. She's gone. Who knows what happened to her? She disappeared. Maybe that's the best way to live here. Make the old you completely disappear."

"I don't know," I said. "You ever thought about it? Coming here to stay?"

"Honestly, I like a life that includes hot showers and television. I could give up drawing my little pictures for that."

We promised to keep in touch regularly, and said our goodbyes. I didn't go any closer to the building that housed the portal, although it didn't seem to matter that much anymore. I made my way east of Droad, to the farming land there, and worked a few weeks in the fields, feeling unused muscles bend, stretch, ache. It's good to make those muscles work every now and again.

Alex stayed true to his promise, for a while. He would find me when I was performing at some event or another, and he would tell me what was happening at Collision. He found out what he could about the new recruits, and I tracked them, monitored their positions on this side. I threw subtle impedances their way, to keep them from reaching influential roles.

Trevor was a different matter. I didn't find him through my tentative enquiries, but then, I have to admit I did not try very hard. This is a big world, but thinking of Trevor made it feel smaller for me. I liked the idea that we could never come across each other, and I think, unconsciously, I aimed for that. Still, I was not wilfully averting my gaze. I started making my own plans against Collision's plans. I cultivated an army of my own. Not among the rich or powerful, but at the roots of life, amongst the very young and idealistic, and the hungry. It was easy to do; I picked out those that served others, moving unseen through the crowds, and I put money in their pockets as part of my act—a cheeky redistribution of wealth that even the wealthy did not seem to mind. I did this for hundreds of youths. I bought their gratitude, and their loyalty, yes, but beyond that, I saw them. I cherished them. I played the odds, thinking that one day I might find one at a serendipitous moment, waiting for me as if born for the task I needed completed. I stand by my actions.

Meanwhile, the cold war grew more heated. Relations were strained between north and south over odd issues such as agriculture. Certain resources were suddenly in short supply for the first time, and each side blamed the other for stockpiling them. Trade negotiations turned sour. The sides demanded more and offered less, and goodwill could not be found. I felt the undercurrents of unease, and began to hear the activation of old rumours: *they hate us, they mean to starve us, they take everything that's good for themselves, they they they...* I tailored my acts towards unity, but the messages of entertainment had somehow been belittled, as if nothing important could come from light pursuits. I blamed Trevor: the unseen bogeyman. Was he pulling strings, or shaking the high wire upon which I balanced?

When things got too bad to ignore I travelled towards the border, looking to see what reparations I could make.

The hills rose, turned to mountains. I travelled as a merchant down on his luck, and caught a lift with a chairmaker, of all things. I sat beside him in his cart, which was filled with his wobbly and unimpressive wares. He told me cheerfully that he was not a good chairmaker, having learned the trade from his father who was also not a good chairmaker, but he hoped practice would make him better, and I agreed that it could not hurt. He was heading for Stravatch, close to the great fortress called Crag on the border, which was the undefeated stronghold of the south, and he said that he had no doubt preparations were underway there. How could it be that everyone had begun to share the same belief at the same time? Were they creating the energy necessary for war, or were they simply commenting on someone else's machinations?

I realised I did not want to see Stravatch, or Crag. I'd had a destination in mind, all along. I left him the following morning and turned to Avock, higher in the mountains—a town I had heard mentioned in association with the Syld. On the northern side of the border.

I crossed without incident. Things had not become so heated yet, then. It gave me hope.

Avock was as I pictured it: small, insular, and in thrall to her. I asked around and met with suspicion. They guarded her jealously. But eventually I was directed to a neat house, surrounded by squat trees. Two incongruously large posts flanked the path, upon which sat big cats carved in stone, both smiling. The garden was well-tended, the windows clean. I wondered if this was her dream of a home. I heard running water close by but couldn't see it.

I thought of the time I had drunk a few pints and visited her flat, standing outside her communal door with my finger on the button of the intercom. I wanted to think that everything about me had changed, but one thing had not: it still felt like a submission to come to her. As if even this had been part of her plan all along.

I hovered there, between the posts, and two men opened the door and came down the path. The shorter one strutted ahead of the taller; they eyeballed me, they were ridiculous. It was a sight that belonged back in Portsmouth, outside a pub past eleven o'clock.

"You looking for someone?" the shorter one said. He had the very blond hair of the east, grown long, collected into a plait over one shoulder. The other one was balding, and looked like more of a threat to me.

"I have a message for the Syld," I said.

"She's not here."

"Is that so?" I aimed to sound mildly interested. "Do you work for her?"

"We keep the house," said the larger one.

"And a good job you do too. All looks in fine order."

He tilted his head. He could not tell if it was a compliment or an insult, perhaps, and I reminded myself to tread carefully. I needed to be memorable, not thumped into oblivion.

"You from the south?" he said.

"I have come from there."

"I thought so." The other one laughed, and I lost my taste for the game.

"I am a trader of eels," I said. "The Syld enquired after the possibility of a basket of my wares from Droad, for a party she plans to hold here, inviting many people of high importance from the south."

Both men frowned. It would be the talk of the town tomorrow, and yes, I wanted to disturb them all, to puncture this protectionist seal she had set up around herself. Could she not simply live her life without bleeding the tactics of her past into her future? No, she could not, and neither could I.

Disgusted at us both, I said to them, "But if my eels are not wanted then I shall go, and not wish you well for my wasted time."

"Watch your tone, friend."

"I am no friend of yours. I came to do business."

"You find such words work with many customers?" said the shorter one, shaking his head at me as if he was my better, and I could see Archie had whispered words to him that had given him airs and graces.

It was so tiring, so ridiculously boring. I simply walked away, away from the house and through the streets of the town, walking without caring where I went for a while. The houses grew smaller, spaced further apart, and the road thinned to a path, then began to wind upwards. The sound of water was still strong around me, and I realised it was coming from the mountains themselves—the melting snow from its peaks streaming down the sides to form underground lakes, maybe, feeding the many black, bushy trees and the sparkling grasses that sprouted on the slopes. It was a beautiful place. They all are, aren't they? They all are.

I found an inn with a pointed roof, four thick wooden tables set up outside, and ordered the plate of the day, which turned out to be thick, nutty cheese melted over slices of an orange vegetable I did not recognise. I couldn't remember eating a better meal, and my mood lifted.

She came down the road I had just travelled, marching at an energetic pace, with a grey cape thrown over her shoulders and her hands deep in the pockets of her trousers. She stopped in front of my table and nodded, as if we had organised this meeting from the beginning.

"They've long been unwelcoming to strangers around here," she said. "It's not my influence alone, I promise. Or the threat they think the south represents, and which I can't seem to talk them out of."

"Are you hungry, Archetta?" I asked her.

"Absolutely." She sat opposite me, her back to the road. How supremely confident she was of her safety. She was older and it suited her: that touch of wisdom in the way she schooled her smile. She seemed easier in her own body. No full-frontal charm assault any longer, no sense of her urgency to dominate. I wondered if she had learned to conserve her energy. The woman who owned the inn came over, and was all delight to see the Syld in her establishment once more; she talked of her new grandchild, and the upcoming cider that was fermenting in her cellar. Then she left to fetch more food. Archie was gracious and warm throughout, and my certainty that it was all still a manipulation was shaken. Why did I not want to believe that she was capable of more? It could only be good news for both of us.

I wanted it to be true, then. But I did not let down my guard.

"You look really well," I said. "Life is suiting you." It sounded odd. A strange expression. I'd got it wrong, somehow.

"I love it here," she said. "I resent the things that take me from my little house."

"You're in demand. The professional partygoer."

"It's a way to make a living."

"Is it all you wanted?"

"I think... yes. It is. And such fulfilment comes at a price. Do you feel that too? I suspect you do, or you wouldn't be here."

"I saw Alex," I said. And I told her of Collision's new cohort of trainees, and Trevor Arklow, here, putting plans in place directly.

"I know," she said. "I have military contacts. He's concerned himself with the south command. In the background, as ever."

"You didn't think to tell me?"

"Marius, I didn't know if you would care. I needed you to come to me."

"Yes, that's what you like, is it not? To hold all the cards."

"Think that if you like, but I tell you now your presence here is the greatest gift I've had in years. It proves to me that there's a chance."

"Of what?"

"Of sorting out the mess we made," she said, and the extra food arrived, and there was more talk of the grandchild. She gave herself to it utterly, and when we left the inn behind I found there was no question in my mind. We needed to be together. For a time.

We walked back in the direction of town together, arms linked.

"I wish there was a way I could sum up how this world is different," she mused. "It's not innocence, or naiveté. And yet…"

"And yet they think nothing will end," I said.

"Or that they do not think they will be the cause of any end."

"It's responsibility. That's the difference."

She squeezed my arm. "Will you stay?"

"For a few days," I said, and I think I was waiting, then, for the beginning of that impossible end—for a portent only Archie and I would recognise.

"Then come home with me, and I'll talk to you as if an aircraft carrier in private hands lies just off the coast and that's no cause for alarm."

"Can you? Talk to me like that? Or have you forgotten the knack of it?"

"Fuckit," she said. The word squeezed out of her, rusty and odd, and we both laughed.

The next days were the best we spent together.

She felt it too, I think.

But I can understand how one feels that way in retrospect, reliving the moment at the cusp of change, hearing tweeting birds build nests in the thick branches of those black trees, even though the season was wrong. Memories are malleable, and they stretch to fit the space we give them. Now I know there will be no more with her, I will breathe into those days of the past, and stretch them out into a lifetime of happiness. Not because we were perfect lovers—love was the least interesting thing we shared—but because we talked in two languages that were the same language, talked of one world and another, and made a third from that mess of intentions. It was a delight of discovery, of companionship, of fresh and deepened understanding. I showed her how some of my tricks worked, slowed my hands and bared my private pockets. She talked to me of where she came from, and how she flew straight and true from that direction. That's one of the few stories I will not deign to tell. I will say she never compromised herself, because she had no high ideals. There was no room for them. Instead she had clung to one certainty—that she should be the centre of the story. Not just her story, but all stories. The brightest star in the sky. Imagine feeling that way since you were little. Imagine being certain that there is no line between your reality and your mind, and nobody else is as vivid. Once I understood that about her, I realised that the mere fact that she tolerated me, allowed me in her presence, was the greatest compliment she could have ever paid me. It should have been enough.

But I could not stand it for long.

I had been right to leave her by the mouth of the river, but this time around I understood my reasoning better. I had to be worth more than what she chose to give me, even though she was very generous by her standards. It did not take more than a few days for that abrasive, coarse difference between us to manifest once more. But we completed our plans for the salvation of this world in good humour, and with hope. We laid out a plan entire, and audacious.

Once it was done, I steeled myself to tell her that I had to leave. A warm autumn swirled around us, leaves falling as we sat in her garden, landing on us, around us. She wore her white fur.

"You still look good in that," I told her.

She thanked me, and said, "I keep it for special occasions, now."

I nodded. So she already knew what I would say, which meant there was no reason to say it.

"Do you remember that board game café in Southsea?" she said. "The one by the Co-op."

For a moment none of it would come back to me. Then, yes, part of my mind unlocked and I saw it, with the shelves at the back stacked high with hundreds of brightly coloured boxes, all a little worse for wear for having been opened and played so many times. The café had served millionaire's shortbread with the coffee, meaning that everything got sticky—the dice, the counters, the tabletops. On Tuesday nights there had been tournaments in a collectible card game I liked as a teenager, with a magic system that appealed, pouring natural resources into a pool of power that could then be divided up to summon creatures or cast spells of fire, water, earth. The cards would still be under my childhood bed. A strange thought. Rusty emotions about my parents surfaced in me. I thrust them back down.

"I used to go there," I said.

"I know. Tuesday nights. I played you, once."

"You played—I don't remember that. You played in the tournaments?"

"I didn't look anything like someone you'd remember."

"You don't get to choose who remembers what, Archie," I said, but she was right again—was she always right? I had no memory of her.

"I didn't place you for the longest time," she said. "Just felt you had one of those faces. Or that I'd known you before. In a different life. Do you know what I mean? It only came to me once we were here, in this world. Since I've lived here, I see Portsmouth differently. I can see every detail of that game café. I can taste the millionaire's shortbread. I see you there, playing your cards close to your chest, wondering what move to make. Before you got muscles. Before you became Marius. One of the reasons I recommended you for the programme was because I felt I knew you, somehow. Just a little."

"And how did you get recommended for it?" I asked her. How had she managed to manoeuvre her way to the centre of Collision? It was a feat more impressive than any I had managed. I began picking up leaves, gathering them in a pile. The sound of water was louder, in that part of the garden; maybe an underground river was directly beneath us.

She ignored the question.

I suppose the answer to it has died with her.

"I'm in a coma," she said. "I'm in the deepest sleep, on the point of death, in Queen Alexandra Hospital, up the hill, in Cosham, and this is the dream."

I touched her arm with a leaf: a gentle stroke.

"All right, then. Portsmouth was never real. I made it up, it's a sickness. That whole world is a sickness that won't ever quite be washed from me."

"Must it be one or the other?" I said.

"I don't think I can hold them in my head any longer. Not both. Not with the plans we have put in place." She leaned forward, curled up on her side, her head in my lap, and I stroked her hair. It was true that we had set ourselves upon a course that was difficult to contemplate. We'd agreed that we had to rid this world of the other, separate them utterly; we would make the new trainees return to the *Iris*, along with Trevor and Alex, and shut the portal behind them. Behind us, too. A return to Portsmouth. A return to grey streets and bin days and the responsibility of having ruined everything natural and good simply by existing.

"You're sure you want to go through with this?"

"I think I must. And you, too. Right?"

"Together or not at all," I said, and I would swear that was the moment when I heard her name being called from the house, and the shorter man from her retinue came running over the grass towards us, his face alight, urgent, despair and disbelief, a letter held in his outstretched hand.

She took the letter and read it aloud. I remember little of the specific wording. It was from a member of the Mutuality at Droad, an old friend of hers. He had been returning to the city from a trip to see relatives, further down the coast. He'd seen a bright light as he reached the hill before the vineyards, too bright to be withstood. He'd covered his eyes. One member of his party had continued to look, had lost his sight. It was yet to come back. Then a great warm wind had blown over them, and he reported feeling thankful for the luck of being in the lee of a hill. Darkness followed, caused by a climbing cloud that billowed out to a flat head, as grey and solid as an anvil. When he climbed the hill, he saw the vineyards destroyed, the houses blown flat. The workers stumbled in the ruins of the fields. He went to help them, and found them dazed, burned red. Something in him said: *Don't go on to Droad.* So he stayed, and helped those workers, and watched their teeth loosen and their fingernails fall out. Some lived. Many died. Others arrived, staggering from the direction of Droad, and said it had flown apart like leaves in a storm. All the great houses, gone. Rubble. Thousands killed. Only tiny pieces remained. Then those survivors died too.

At the end of the letter he wrote: *Why Droad? It was the heart of us all.*

She folded up the letter.

"Thank you, Bell," she said, and the man burst into tears. His misery was awful. She got up, patted his arm. "Tea for all, I think," she said, and led us back to the kitchen where she made the drinks herself.

I understood then what she meant about the irreality of knowledge. How could Droad be gone? And yet we both knew the answer to that. We knew that a weapon existed that could level cities, and somehow it had been loosed. Not by the north or the south, but by the malevolent presence of our own world. Our leaders had not dared to detonate it on their soil, but perhaps they were unbothered about the consequences of their actions upon this land. Or one of the terrorist organisations Alex had told me about had done it. This was the kind of thing terrorists did.

But as we drank our tea, sitting in silence, the whole household as one, it occurred to me that this might not be a one-off incident at all. Could it be that HMS *Iris*, the entirety of Portsmouth, had been destroyed? Did war rage in the place of my birth? Across all the tensions and rivalries I had grown up with? Countries, factions, religions, hatreds. And the gamblers, of course, the gamblers wanting their returns. I could imagine them betting on this outcome. Backing who would live and who would die.

Archie sipped her tea and would not look at me. I could tell she was thinking the same things. All the plans we had already made were now useless.

We finished the tea, and she hugged everyone tight, giving gentle words, patting hands. I recognised a soft look in her eye that I used to see when she looked at images on her phone, never far from her hand, of puppies, or baby bears in the woods. Eventually we retired to her chamber, although it was not yet dark, and she asked all her staff not to disturb her as we worked through the new permutations of the future, as we saw them.

In one way the use of a weapon of mass destruction did simplify things. The portal could not have survived the blast, so Collision no longer had a way into this world. And our goal remained the same: to rid this world of our kind.

"We must not be predictable," she mused, "not obvious. We must infiltrate in surprising ways so that Trevor and the others cannot see us coming. They'll count us as a threat, of course. If they think we've teamed up, if they get even a sniff of our agenda, they'll look to neutralise us. How do we throw them off the scent?"

"We split up," I said.

Her room was very plain. The white fur lay on the coverlet of the small, simple bed, and she sat in the seat of the bay window, on a row of grey cushions. All the other rooms in her house were ornate in decoration, each piece presented to prompt a charming recollection, such as the time she'd travelled to a certain place, or met a certain person. She could entertain for hours that way. Of course, they were for show. But this room offered no show. It was empty. Different from that small flat she had kept in Southsea. Perhaps she had learned to find peace in emptiness. I was glad. I thought it might make our plans easier to carry out, like travelling light upon a dangerous road. I said, "They'll assume we'd stay together. Or, if not that, then you'd go north, to the mountains, and I'd go south. So we do the opposite. And we persuade them in the way that it's done that we have become enemies."

She put a hand to her forehead, rubbed the place between her eyes, and I wondered if she was saddened by the idea of separation. "It makes sense," she said.

"Let's assume Alex and the new trainees were too far down the pecking order of Collision employees to know anything useful, such as a possible attack or an internal scheme that carried a risk. Chances are they were in Droad when…" I swallowed. "I will travel that way, get as close as I dare, try to check for them. If they are all dead, that makes our job easier." I felt my legs shiver, wanted to sit, but I did not dare. I had to keep moving. I paced the bare floorboards, then practised some balancing exercises as I spoke on, standing on one leg then the other, holding out my arms as if on the wire once more. "Then I'll go to the mountains and offer my services to the north. Do you have trustworthy contacts there? Someone who'll vouch for me, get me in? We'll need a way to stay in touch."

She nodded. "I'll write it down. You can memorise it."

"What haven't we thought of?"

"Trevor," she said.

"Yes. Trevor."

"He'll be wary of us. Determined not to let us get close, particularly if he's in an influential position. I'll work out a way to reach him. But it's not enough to reach him: we need him to talk, too. To tell us what he knows, so we're sure we've got everyone."

"I'll leave it in your capable hands."

"To be clear," she said. "We are talking about making sure everyone from our world who has come into this world is dead. Every single one. If they aren't dead, we have to kill them."

"Yes. Is that too plain? Would you prefer something about putting right our mistakes? You've framed it that way before."

"Maybe that's too moralistic for my taste right now, with Droad a pile of ash. One hopes moral choices involve less of a body count."

"Is this not the moral path, then?"

"I'll get back to you when we reach the end," she said, then, "Trevor, yes, Trevor will be difficult. It'll take years to convince him we're not working together. I hope you're in this for the long haul."

"Absolutely." I was reassuring myself as much as her, but yes, it was true, we would be enemies, ostensibly, for a long time, and I had no clue if I could trust her or myself.

"Have you killed people before?" she asked me.

"No."

"Are you sure you can?" I don't think she meant to be condescending, although she had past form in that. It was simply to make sure I had the necessary skills, including the mindset.

"Honestly, Archie, I don't know. But since they've blown up my favourite city I'm prepared to give it a go." It sounded so Portsmouth that we both laughed, a surprising sound, and I thought: *We were healing, we were on the path to being healed and this has undone it all, and we are now damaged beyond repair.* I said, "This is our last night together, then."

Her mouth twitched "You want romance?"

"I want you to tell me that we are unbreakable allies over distance and time. Agreed?"

"Agreed."

This will sound strange, but we spat on our hands and shook on it. Then we went to bed.

The next eight years of my life, in a nutshell, for we approach the end of this voyage: I became a patriot of the north, and I became a killer. Funny how well these two things fitted together. I won't go through the details of it. Alex and two of the trainees, I think, were in Droad when it was blown to rubble. I found no further sign of them. The other two trainees, I murdered. I was a different man after these acts. And I murdered more people besides, as is expected of one who picks a side in a war. I learned how time and experience change a person, and I suffered the nightmares and flashbacks that only seemed fair. A dread settled over me, but I remembered how I had changed before, from Miles to Marius, and I wondered if I would change again before the end.

The massing of troops began. It would have been pointless to attempt to stop the game of blame and hatred that erupted. I felt a giant machine was working against me, filling all the ears it could reach with vitriolic lies. I did not try to influence the war, but maintain my own standing as an elusive, wondrous figure. I spread stories tailored to that end. One builds a reputation as a great spy not by doing the job, but by making others think you are doing it well. After all, the point of real espionage is to go unnoticed, and I needed to stay visible. Occasionally I would reach a town and find that a new rumour about my ability to appear, disappear, charm and kill, had arrived before me. I put this down to Archie, hard at work too, and I spoke of her in return. I cast her as my greatest foe.

The strongest opposing pieces on the gameboard can appear to be involved under a different set of rules, playing only against each other. I liked the thought of how it would look to others: the Allynx Syld and the Misheard Word, operating at a level beyond normal comprehension. And, very occasionally, rumours, only whispered, at the highest level: the Oster, the mastermind behind it all.

And so it was.

And so we come to Crag.

Crag, that historied rock-hewn bastion that dated back into the dim battles of the past. What a feat of effort it must have taken to carve it from the mountain.

I wish I had seen it for the first time under different circumstances.

Word came from Archie that she had devised a plan to reach Trevor within Crag—*that monstrosity made from nature,* she called it, in her letter, and I did not know if she referred to the prison or the man we sought within it. I travelled to the border under the guise of a supply waggoner, taking food to the front. It was a slow journey with my donkey; unimpressed by my reputation, she could not be charmed to move faster. People I met along the way were jittery. The war was beginning to bite hard. I heard reports of atrocities that seemed beyond unlikely to me; it had never been in the nature of this world to commit such acts. I put it down to Trevor's influence, spreading propaganda, although to what ends I could not say.

On the stalemate of the front line, youths sat and played dice and waited to age or die, whatever came first. Stravatch, still under control of the south, was not far. Under the cover of night I crossed the border, slipped inside. Found the house of the chairmaker I had once travelled with, followed him on a rainy night to his local tavern and sat upon the stool next to him for a time until he looked up and recognised me, and I recognised him back. Such apparent serendipity is powerful, particularly when it feels like fate is against you. He was delighted to remember better times with me, and invited me to stay at his house, apologising for the lack of room. A relative of his wife, a great uncle, had been staying with them and tutoring his children. Would I be content with a pallet by the fire, he asked me? I told him I had lost my own bed and family: a pallet by a warm hearth would be the best of lodgings. Our friendship and his loyalty secured, he took me home with him.

One look at his kitchen told me that he hadn't improved his carpentry skills much. Maybe life—being a husband, a father—had distracted him. I perched on a wobbly stool and charmed his wife, complimented his children. His eldest son also worked in the carpentry business, but now they specialised in crates and had a hefty contract with the military. It was a merry little oasis to find in a difficult time.

"And this is Master Fider," he told me, and an aged man with a wild grey thatch of hair and mournful eyes came into the kitchen, wearing the over-robe of an academic, although it was tatty and tired. Fider took up a plate and helped himself to boiled vegetables from the platter in the centre of the table. He had a strong smell of wine about him, wafting from his robe as he leaned over me. Once he was seated opposite, lowering himself gently on to the wobbly stool, I asked how he fared. The chairmaker had told me the man was at the destruction of Droad. I wished to enquire after his health, whether he had lost teeth or hair, how he suffered, but that would not suit dinner table conversation, so I hoped to prompt him a little.

"I keep myself busy," he said. "I look for talent in the young, and try to nurse it." The look he gave the two children of the chairmaker suggested he did not think he had found it there. They ignored him merrily and asked to be excused. As they left the table I asked him, "You have done that for many years, sir?"

"Many. And my pupils should now be out in the world making it a better one, but all I cultivated were taken from me in a moment. I was at Droad, I saw what happened. I will never get over it."

"You saw it with your own eyes?"

"I was close," he said. "I was very close, only a twist of fate meant I had travelled upriver to swim at the Farelem waterfalls that day, for my health. I saw the light in the sky and some instinct told me to dive. I'd read, in an old book, about great explosions of long past battles, and how people fled to water. Learning is often underrated, my friend, but I think it saved me that day. If only there could have been a way to save Droad… Damn this war, damn it. But does it suit you, sir? Do you make money from it?"

"I make money where I must, but I am no friend of it, or of the circumstances that led to it. I knew Droad very well. I miss it more than I can say."

"As do I," he said. "As do I. We can never go back, in time or in place, can we? All the knowledge in the world will not allow either of those wishes to come true, and I—I feel as if a great evil has come among us. I have studied... looked for clues..."

The chairmaker rolled his eyes. I guessed he had heard this many times before.

Two things came to me: Master Fider was drunk, and he was also desperate. A useful combination, and I had no backup plan in place. I listened to him, agreed with him, and once the chairmaker and his wife had given up and retired for the evening I began to feed Fider stories. Much like my army of youths, planted in unexpected places, I made a tool of Fider. The only difference was that this time I did not have to lie to do it.

I remember seeing the light of belief, of revelation, burn strong in his sotted eyes. I felt nothing. The end of the mission was finally in sight—what matter an old man's mind, as one more casualty? I said to him:

You are right, you have always been right. I must tell you, you are a wise man to see what so many have refused to face, but the evidence is overwhelming, yes, you have been infiltrated. Your world is compromised. It is a plaything, a battleground, for evil. For an alien race so advanced in technology that they have found a way to come among you, to use you to amuse themselves, and they do not care who gets hurt. The power that destroyed Droad: of course it did not come from your own people, good and kind and true. You only have to trust your own wisdom to know that to be so. And how do I know this? For I am many things. I am Mondegreen, the Misheard Word. And I am one of those aliens, who now walks among you. There are more of us. We fight our own war, on your soil. Some of us want to live in peace, and others—others must be stopped. Can you help? Will you help? I ask it humbly of you. Help me to end this secret invasion, and I promise you, I will make sure all of us leave your world for good, and for ever. But I cannot do this without you.

Good old Master Fider. He brought out the worst in me at the best possible time.

I spent two days with the chairmaker and his exceptionally average, hugely blessed family. I winked theatrically at Fider and suggested a number of courses of action, hoping one would trigger in certain circumstances. There, I will admit, I got lucky.

Then, at the third bell of the third day, I strolled down to Stravatch dock and stood before the green light of the quay, until Archie's underlings leapt out from behind a conveniently placed wall of cargo to capture me.

Only once they had me wrapped up tight in rope, my mouth gagged, did Archie come out from her hiding place to stand before me. Eight years had passed since I'd last seen her.

"Marius!" she said. "Finally, I have you exactly as I want you. And I know precisely what to do with you, too." She played it very well. Dramatic, but the war had brought out that side in people. She was wonderful to look upon, in the full throes of a performance upon a performance; who knew where either of us really lay, anymore? *Miles is dead,* I thought. *Archie is dead. We will not use those names again. The journey is ending.*

She gloated, she exulted. A victory for the south. I was crated to be sent to Crag, as a gift to Warden Beck. The wood of the crate was very rough, and it was badly made. I thought I detected the work of my happy chairmaker.

We had stacked the odds in our favour. We thought the chances were strong that we could rid this world of the influence of Collision by playing upon the Oster's weaknesses, then forcing him to reveal the extent of our world's infiltration.

But the game did not resolve as we wanted.

And so here I am, sailing to Droad with you. You, Elize Janview, a member of a private army I created, who could not follow the simplest prompt and present yourself at the Syld's chambers at the right time. Something went wrong. We do not have our answers as to what Collision planned, what Trevor aimed for. And Archetta no longer cares, one way or another.

So we will travel to Droad, you and I.

We will check that no sign of my world exists in yours.

And then you will make sure that I die.

BOOK THREE
CHASM

CHAPTER TWENTY-ONE

DO STORIES ONLY influence the listener when there is perfect understanding?

I spent three weeks on the road with Mondegreen after that fateful flight from Crag. I puzzled over the tale he had told me. I felt certain he had meant every word of it, but what did those words mean? What did they become, when strung together?

The Misheard Word. He spoke, and I did not have the ears to hear his meaning. Something in my nature—the distance between his world and mine—prevented me from making sense of it all, and so it would stay half-sketched to me, despite all the dark colour and intent he had tried to breathe into it.

At least there was no doubt that he was leading us back to Droad. He knew the journey as well as I did. He kept to older lanes that ran parallel to the bigger trade routes, and had an innate sense of direction that meant he could plunge into scrubland or bushes if others appeared ahead, cutting across land to emerge back on the lane once they had passed. It amazed me that someone not born to this world could manage such a thing. At times, when I followed behind him, watching the back of his untucked, grimy shirt and the fall of his unkempt hair, I would wonder why I did not simply stop moving. Or I could have swung to another direction, found my own way. But still I kept pace, and he never checked. He assumed I would be there, and when we came to the end of each day's walking, or paused to collect apples, not quite ripe, or found berry bushes or a fresh spring, he would look upon me very directly. He would offer me food or water, or pat the ground beside him, and I would hold his hand, or his gaze.

A wondrous thing, that gaze. I had been starved of it, told I could not ever have it, and now I could not get enough. I felt he had some wild power that came from his world alone: the ability to charm, to sway others to belief. Isn't that what had happened? Was still happening?

Midsummer. The nights were short and the weather easy for travelling. The war had been left behind us, and I found myself thinking that Droad must be intact, just up ahead, busy and bright with events planned in the Mutuality's halls, such as the Harvest Hatted Dance. The ballroom would be decorated with ribbons and knotted corn to match the market stalls, and Vella Iffluce would open its gardens and serve cool tea on the lawn to everyone, rich and poor alike. It was not a perfect city. It had its criminals and its corruptions. But it was better than most, I did believe that. Where else could the daughter of a servant find her pocket full of money, and use it to buy a new way through life? Blessed. I was blessed, and so was Droad.

Except it was dead.

It was hard to keep in my mind as the land we walked became ever more familiar. Here was the sheltering dollie that marked the outskirts of the city fields: a slab of stone propped up by two others, and the traditional way survived here—dry kindling had been left for whoever might need its harbour. And here was a stream that crossed and curved and swelled before tumbling into a pool that I thought I knew. We stopped, and washed, separately, although we did not break our gaze. I saw how the time of enforced stillness in the pinnacle had taken its toll on his muscles, and he was lean, and stretched tight across his chest and his thighs. I wondered how I looked to him, but I did not ask. It was enough to be seen. And here was, eventually, on the third week of walking, a stretch of farmland that I felt utterly sure of. Grapes were growing, small clusters of them that would thicken over summer, but the vines were already bowing under the weight. The farmhouses were squat and singular, bunched together for all who worked this stretch. We passed at dusk; there were yellow candles in the windows. Inside, they would be eating their shared meal, then singing or playing games until tiredness overtook them. It would be a good year, I guessed, with wonderful wine to come.

CHAPTER TWENTY-TWO

"POISONED," SAID MONDEGREEN. "All of it. Not just the grapes. Everything that comes from Droad. Everything we see, The weapon has left it all poisoned, for hundreds of years, maybe."

We had settled in a small wooden barn for the night, further on from the farmhouses and tucked away behind an overgrown copse so it was barely visible from the track. It was a forgotten place, and there was nothing inside but a collection of rusted scythe blades in one corner, a sack of mouldy meal beside them, and thick nests of long-vacant cobwebs in the eaves. Even the spiders had moved on.

Its abandonment seemed to suit Mondegreen's mood. He had smiled, bade me lay down the Syld's fur so we could sit side by side upon it as had become our habit. There were only a few shards of moonlight falling through the slits in the walls and roof, where the weeds did not reach. I could see the long line of his nose, the hollow of his cheek. He was more fragrant, and revived for his wash in the pool. I put my hand to his forehead and stroked back his tangled hair. I sensed this was a good moment to ask my questions. There was a relaxation in him that could indicate a willingness to speak once more of the things left behind.

"Does that mean the objects I unearthed from Droad and brought to the pinnacle were poisoned too?"

"It does." He sighed. "It was not part of my plan, but it forced Trevor's hand effectively, did it not? He had to know if we had found whatever it was he sought from the wreckage. He had to confront Archetta."

"But we sat with them. We touched them. We are poisoned too." It was difficult to say. I swallowed, then asked, "How could a weapon do that?"

"I don't know. Something to do with the ripping apart of the tiny elements that make up all things."

"Fire, earth, water?"

"I'm not a scientist, I can't…" His voice died away.

"Will we die soon?" I said.

"I do not know, and honestly, I am sorry. But I need an audience. Can you understand that?"

"I… think your people care only for themselves."

"You and me both," he said. "But still, who knows how long anyone has? It might take days, weeks, years. Maybe it will not affect you at all. Maybe the poison has already spread throughout this land, and they are all walking corpses who do not know it yet. Or maybe it will affect the children, or the children who come after that." He took my hand, stroked the back of it with his thumb. "Do not have children, Elize. Just to be safe."

I took my hand from his. I closed my eyes and tried to bring my mother's face to mind. It would not come. It was one loss too many.

"Why do you cry?" he asked, and the astonishment in his voice cut me. I couldn't reply, had to wait for the moment to pass. It did, as all moments do, and I said, "I cannot recall my mother's face."

"Faces are overrated," he said. "Think *around* the face. What was her work?"

"She was a cook."

"A good profession. Picture her working dough. You will have seen that often, but not tried to hold it so tightly."

He was right. There she was, in my mind's eye, flour on her hands, that particular line to her shoulders as she kneaded with her cheerful efficiency, with one of her cheap necklaces—the one of red glass beads—bouncing on her throat. The spacious kitchen of the Mutuality thrived around her, and she was the centre of its noise, its colour. She was alive.

"Tell me," he whispered, so I described her. At first I had her with me, guiding my words, but the more I spoke the more she receded, and soon she was pale and blurred, and I stopped talking, afraid of losing her entirely once more.

"You would both kill me and walk away without a glance," I said. It was a horror that I could not fathom. I was disappearing too, vanishing into his indifference. But his eyes said otherwise, did they not? He had to keep looking at me. He had to.

"I don't think anything can kill you, Elize."

"You think me invincible?" The idea cheered me up for a moment, then crumbled into pieces jagged, difficult to hold. "How could I be? Do I seem so different to you?"

"It's not you," he said. "It's me." He said it automatically, without emotion. Then smiled. Then he said:

There were once two friends who were sealed up tight in a box that had been devised by their worst enemies. The air was running out inside this box. They could hear their enemies through the walls, many of them, in dispassionate discussion. They commented on what they thought was happening inside the box.

"Surely one has attacked the other by now," someone said. "One less pair of lungs to take up what air is left."

"I think they are caught in a moment of high emotion," said another, "and they make love, writhing together naked on the floor."

"The air will have run out by now," said a third. "They are already dead, take my word for it."

"You think so? I'll take that bet."

"Let's see your money."

The two friends in the box sat side by side, and waited. They knew nothing would happen to them before the game of betting on the outcome was concluded, for who can have real emotions or actions in an unreal environment? So they kept their patience, being neither alive nor dead, neither lovers nor haters, until they heard the creak of the front panel of the box being levered free, and then they—

A voice, outside. A voice I recognised.

Mondegreen fell silent.

I moved into a crouch, then straightened, crossed to the wall. I put my eye to one of the slits between the logs, and it gave me a slim view, surrounded by leaves, of the dirt track, passing by.

There he was, striding fast, setting a pace. Unmistakeable. Warden Beck.

He stopped, called over his shoulder. "Did you not hear me? Come on. Faster." His head was angled towards the barn, surely he could see it? I felt exposed, my eye to the wood. No, he did not see it. He moved on.

Then, along the track, two soldiers I recognised. I did not recall their names, had never shared a shift with them, but they were from Crag. I could place them in the long hall, up by the fire, keen to share their tales of woe and drink up the warmth. They looked grimy, dejected. They each held a rifle, and walked in step. Not quite a march. But Beck compelled them, and they obeyed.

Behind them, excluded from their rhythm, was Tommo's friend—the one who had guarded the long room on the night of the arrival of the refugees from Stravatch. What was her name? Starke. I held my breath. Was Tommo with her? Just a few steps behind? He could have survived the beach, become the new Beck for the modern age...

He did not appear.

Starke's expression should have told me as much. I would not see Tommo again.

"It's not a question of bravery."

Beck's voice had been a shock, but this voice raised emotions in me that I could barely control. I put my hands to my mouth as Master Fider took his time down the track. He wore a short cloak that looked too small for him. I wondered where he had found it. There was blood on this side of his face, dried in a rivulet from a sticky wound in the wild nest of his hair. "It's the presence of a superior being," he was saying. His voice carried clearly.

A sharp breath in came from Mondegreen, close to my ear. I had been so focused on the passage of this remnant force from Crag that I had not been aware of his presence beside me. He had put his face to another chink in the wall, was observing the scene before us.

"Do not see us," he whispered.

"It's the understanding that we are not alone in this world and that our shared history is a series of untruths designed to keep us compliant so they can play their games."

"Want to bet on that?" said Imberley. There she was, walking a little behind Fider. She was not in uniform—no, wait, it was a uniform with the jacket removed and the sleeves rolled high, with the trousers cut off below both knees. It looked too big for her. I wondered what had led to this change of outfit. I knew her expressions well, having tried to read them so often as part of our gameplay, and she was not even trying to hide this one—Fider was boring her witless. I guessed the only reason she walked with him was on Beck's order. She was Fider's guard, then. He was under arrest.

Not one of them even glanced in our direction. They walked past, and were gone from our limited sight: a small party, an odd one. Perhaps the only one, apart from ourselves, to escape from the fall of Crag.

CHAPTER TWENTY-THREE

MONDEGREEN STEPPED BACK from the wall and breathed out. "There," he said, as if he had kept the barn hidden from them by cloaking it with his mind, somehow.

"We were lucky," I said.

"It will not take them long to work out they've lost us. Come. We'll skirt around, try to beat them to Droad."

"You think they're searching for you?"

"For us. You lied to the guards, did you not? You are absent without leave. Trevor and Archie are dead, and you are alive and travelling with me. No doubt they think us both agents of the north, if Fider has not managed to persuade them all of something more bizarre. We must push on through the night."

I retrieved the fur from the ground, threw it over my shoulder, and Mondegreen led the way, pushing through the bushes around the barn to emerge with the vineyards behind us and the track out of sight.

I could hardly keep up with him. He did not try to hide. He strode tall, in that mix of dark and light of midsummer evening, and I stumbled along behind, catching every root and weed with my boots. I thought of Imberley's expression as she had listened to Fider, and I wished I could apologise for him, say: *He was a brilliant man, once.* But I could no longer be certain if that had been a mistaken perception on my part, from a time when I was so young, so desperate to find a way to escape a life without answers. I realised I had grasped at the only possibility that had come along.

I had been determined to free myself from Droad.

Droad had been beautiful, yes: a city of gorgeous sights and thriving industries, of sea and garden, of food and wine. My mother had been content, I think, with her three necklaces and her hands shaping bread. Her death, the death of Droad, had been a terrible loss, but it had also simplified, flattened, difficult emotions. It had left me free to love both with my whole heart, as I never had to wrestle free of either. The job was done for me.

The lines, all lines, were blurred. I could not see what I had caused, and what had been done to me, and he never slowed for me, never turned. Beck and his procession were close, blaming me as they blamed Mondegreen, calling us both by that smooth and easy word: enemy.

We reached a stretch of corun, still green. It would take late summer sun to turn them golden. Poisoned. But he showed no hesitation in pushing through them, deep into their cover. They swallowed him and I called, "Wait!" I ran to catch him up, then grabbed the hem of his shirt, and fell into step. He talked to himself. I could hear only the murmur of his voice in the rustle of the corun, not the meaning.

Long dry leaves peeled back from the stems, and I saw, on the vegetable growth itself, a thick grey mould, in patches, and a wet smell of rot. I shrank back from the whispery touch of the leaves, but could not avoid them. They stroked me, and with my hands on Mondegreen's shirt I could not fend them off. I breathed shallow, keeping my lips tightly closed. He did not falter in his direction, and as suddenly as we had come across the corun we were past it, stepping out upon the crest of a hillock with an unimpeded view down to the sea.

I let go of his shirt and came to stand next to him. We linked hands.

The moonlight illuminated a scene that should have belonged only in the imagination: a pen-and-ink rendering of a blasted landscape. I could see where Droad had nestled, between fields and water, growing up from the contours of the ground, but it was not there, and the shape of the land itself had been changed, falling inwards, bubbling up and cracking away, like the remains of a ferocious fire, raked violently, all charred, then scattered by winds. And yet I could still see where the streets had led, met, crossed. I could see where the library had stood, and the gardens of Vella Iffluce, perfect for strolling. And there, jutting up like a broken tooth, was the Mutuality—what was left of it. Three sides collapsed, one remaining with part of a dome curving out, cracked glass catching the moonlight. Between that and the sea, the bridge still stood, spanning the river mouth, and it was unbelievable in its delicacy, its longevity. Some things had survived the weapon. Beyond the bridge, the sea, of course—the indestructible sea, familiar, whole and tamely tied to the shore.

The chasm itself was a black seam through that sight, running from one side of the city to the other, widest at the point where the market had once stood. The land rose to it slightly, puckered to form open lips.

"Is it as you imagined?" said Mondegreen.

"I did not picture it," I said. "I could not have pictured it."

"From now on, when you hear the word Droad, you will see this. The hole where something you love should be. It can never be so simple again."

"It was not uncomplicated anyway," I told him. "Why do you imagine that everything I think and feel is uncomplicated?"

He said, "We can make it by morning," and set off, down into the ruined city, and still I followed.

CHAPTER TWENTY-FOUR

WE LEFT THE smooth land behind. We reached the outskirts where I could recall small houses that once jostled together: a cheerful street, everyone making do. Droad had contained many cultures, many forms of mutual thriving, each one a bubble touching the other. Abandoned. There were signs planted among the rubble:

DANGER TO LIFE
BAD LAND, UNCLEAN WATER
STAY AWAY

But the ruins did thrive, in their own way, with plant growth, and even patches of thick, leathery fungi that I would not have dared to eat. They squatted on the snapped and fallen trunks of trees, and once I had seen them, I began to notice signs of the lives that were still being lived there too. This was not an abandoned place, no matter the warning of the signs. There were the telltale tatters of detritus that came with living the poorest of lives, scavenging on what was left behind. I saw nobody directly, but would sometimes catch a movement: a withdrawal from my peripheral vision, slow and cautious. Yes, people lived here. I was grateful for their decision not to approach us, but to let us pass. I felt afraid of how they might have looked, too—missing teeth, hair, or without lips or eyelids, burned away to rigid grins and stares? I'd heard of such things. Maybe these injuries were also coming to me.

We reached the near lip of the chasm before dawn, stopping a few yards from its edge, upon a plateau of stone that I felt certain had once been the foundations of a trading house. Mondegreen had set a breakneck pace, and I had passed exhaustion into a numb acceptance. The difficulty was not in continuing to walk, but in managing to come to a halt and not fall where I stood. But we had found our way to the chasm. There was no place else to go. I somehow managed to stay on my feet, swaying with the effort.

The drop into the dark ran raggedly across the market—wiped clean by the blast—down to the street that once led to Vella Iffluce. It joined, like a seam, to the start of the bridge, then to the sea. Inland, it curved back on itself and stretched far, too far to see its end.

"Let us wait until sunrise," said Mondegreen.

"For what? To decide whether to die?" I was too tired for anything but the most direct questions. He had promised me he would die here, and I would have seen justice done to those who led to the death of my mother.

"If I say not—would you kill me?" he asked. He sat down on the stone, then laid out flat.

I came to him, put down the fur and laid by his side. A soft wind passed over us. It came from the chasm, perhaps, and it smelled of something unfamiliar, smoky and sweet in equal measure.

"No answer to that?" he said. He turned his head to me, and we locked our gaze. He saw me. "Speak," he said. "Why won't you speak?"

"I can conjure nothing that's worth hearing," I said. "I have spent eight years chasing a dream of revenge, and I have only empty hands to show for it."

He reached down, took my hand again. "Not so."

"I think... I think I want what you want."

"And what is that?"

"A decent end."

He pressed his lips together, half-closed his eyes. He said, "Is my shitshow of a world even there anymore? It was easier with Archetta beside me, holding it all together, being the proof I needed and the impetus to finish what we started. But it's that doubt—that gap where she should be—that drives me now. What is alive over there, and what is dead? Is war everywhere, and have these weapons been unleashed upon all the cities that stood? My parents: are they alive? I used to be certain of it. They were alive, and I had to find some place to exist where they were not. But what if the bungalow in Cosham is gone? What if that way of living is no more? I no longer have to exist to spite it. And so we come to it. For all our fine talk, Archetta and I, of purifying this world from our own malign influence, it turns out all I really wanted was to go home every now and again to check if I still needed to not be there."

"You cannot go home," I told him.

He closed his eyes fully and breathed, deeply. The breathing slowed.

I poked him in the ribs. "Don't sleep."

"I wasn't going to."

"You were on the verge."

"I was not. Aren't you tired, Elize?"

"I'm so tired I cannot see straight."

"But your eyes are very clear. Why are your eyes always so clear? It's as if…"

"What?"

"You look like this land. You both look untouched. Even in the midst of the harm I do to you both, you look untouched. Young."

"I'm twenty-four," I said. "Hardly a baby. And our history

books date back thousands of years. The north, the south, and so on, and so on. We are perhaps older than you."

"Or perhaps your books are—much like our history books—also a lie."

I saw a thought come to him, a powerful one. His gaze did not move, but he was no longer seeing me. Then he dropped my hand, got to his feet, and looked this way and that, at the rubble, the piles of broken brick and splintered wood. "Where are they?" he said, to himself, I think.

"What?"

"Look everywhere. Look hard."

I stood, made a show of examining our surroundings, but I could not help. I had no idea what I was looking for.

"They can work wonders," he said. "They can do anything. I've been a fool. We are fools."

I could see the grainy brightening of the sky over the sea. The sun would soon rise. I said, "There's nothing."

"There must be."

"What?" I said again, in desperation. I felt language slipping away from me, into the hole between us. He ran from side to side, he turned over bricks, dirt, he searched thick clumps of dusty grass and pushed back weeds.

"Cameras," he said.

I remembered the word. The seeing device, from one world to the next. "Would they not all be destroyed? What are they made of?"

He crossed to the lip of the chasm, threw his arms wide, and called, "Game over! Game over!" The sound caught in the crack, reverberated, and a shock of small birds took off close by, moving inland as one. The sky was aglow—the first cast of the sun over the sea had been made, and it seemed to me, for one moment, that Droad was restored by the touch of the light, returned to its tall beauty born of north and south. We stood in the market, whole, busy, traders setting up for the day, pulling their blankets from the wood while fishermen arrived with eels freshly caught, each carrying a box containing a glistening knot of bodies: abundant, salty, many creatures turned into one mass. And the customers, I saw them, the early risers, keen for bargains. I saw my mother at the jewellery stall, exclaiming over the colours, the shapes, and beside her was a child, and the child carried a very small box of her own, made of rough wood, and the child was me.

That had never happened. I had never found a cube, been given a string of beads. The real and the unreal were bleeding together, and neither could be trusted.

"Game over, game over!" Mondegreen shouted into the darkness.

The vision faded.

Droad was dead, my mother was dead, all was dead. I opened my hands, and let fall whatever it was I had been holding all that time: revenge, justice, sorrow. I let it fall.

"Look. Down there."

Mondegreen leaned over the lip, attention fixed on the chasm. Too close; but of course a great height would not scare him. I approached, getting as close as I dared, paces behind him. I saw packed dirt strewn with roots, naked and exposed, as if sheared. I saw a tangle of clothes stuck in mud, broken shards of pottery, many objects that looked just like the ones I had retrieved from the twelfth floor of Crag. They were layered through the sides of the chasm, dropping down further and further to where the sun could not reach, and nothing could be seen. From there, a profound darkness. Impenetrable.

"It looks grainy," he said. "Like sand."

A voice, behind us. "Hold!"

Beck. Beck, the very voice of command: hard, peremptory. Expecting obeisance. Beck led the way over the rubble. Imberley and the others were in his wake. We had not left them behind, and they could not be escaped this time.

"Hold!" Beck called again, his voice rising to a note of desperation I did not understand. An explosion of birds erupted from the emptied shell of the buildings behind him. He turned, watched them rise high, in their panic. We all watched them go.

I turned to Mondegreen. He was gone.

He was not there.

I took a step closer to the lip. The darkness was undisturbed. I looked around me once more, then up and at the sky, at the path the birds had taken.

"Janview," Beck called. "Step back." He slowed his pace, came towards me softly, one hand outstretched. "You are not in trouble. Step back."

Behind him, Imberley's face was a strange picture, her mouth pressed into a fixed line, her eyes wide. I remembered the time she had mimicked a noose around my neck, tongue lolling, standing on tiptoe. She had been wrong then and she was wrong now. I wanted to tell her that. She had already lost the bet anyway. Pappas and Tommo were gone. I could only run a distant third.

I walked towards her with much to say, and I felt Beck's hand on my shoulder, shoving me down as I passed him. I fell to the ground. The two soldiers I did not know were upon me, pinning me with such ease that the breath was knocked from me, the breath and the will to speak lost, and Fider cried, "Gentle, I beg you, gentle," as if I was precious, even though everything good in me had been broken.

CHAPTER TWENTY-FIVE

"PERHAPS IT WAS a northern lie," Beck said. "Or perhaps a sickness that has now cleared. Whatever it was, the poison that tainted this land is gone. Look around. Things grow, and we are in no danger. We'll camp here tonight, then head to the front. With Stravatch and Crag lost, higher command will have moved eastwards."

I said nothing. It was easy to do. I had spent weeks saying nothing, at his command. It seemed hypocritical that he now wanted me to talk. The day had been a long round of questions, and I could answer none of them. No, it came very easily to say nothing at all.

I was propped against an overturned crate, close to the flat stone where Mondegreen and I had laid, side by side, only hours earlier. It was early evening. Beck had ordered a fire built on that stone, and one of the soldiers had gone on the hunt for food. My hands were tied before me, at the wrists, the rope rubbing my skin. Fider was beside me, pulling at his cloak, making sounds of misery. They did not bother to bind him, I noticed.

"Starke, you have first shift," Beck was saying, as the others fed the fire, and cut up foraged wrinkled apples to feed themselves. "Imberley, second. I'll take the shift of the coldest hours. Then Tredd. Zweckel, you have until dawn, and then you'll be on prisoner duty. Make the most of your sleep."

Zweckel, the woman who looked barely out of her schooling years, saluted.

"Sir, I don't think Janview is well," Imberley said, and Beck replied, "Yes, I agree, an illness of the mind, not of the body. I thought she could withstand Mondegreen's powers if he could not speak to her, look at her, but I was mistaken. She has not been in control of her actions for many weeks, I would guess. But she will improve, now she is free of him."

"Will—will she receive care?"

"I'll make sure she is evaluated, and that all is taken into account for her court martial, including my own failings," Beck said. Fider moaned, but he was not a military man and I did not expect him to understand. Of course there would be a trial. I had done something terrible, although I was not certain precisely what that was. Perhaps it was losing the fur of the

Allynx. For it had somehow slipped from my shoulders and was gone, not anywhere within my sight. If I had been about to say anything at all, it would have been to ask the others to search for it. Not to be freed, not to look for myself. But it had to be close. It had been warm around my back and arms at the lip of the chasm, at the very moment of Mondegreen's disappearance. I was sure of it.

Beck came to stand over me once more. He leaned forward, his hands on his knees, and I saw the grimace he pulled. His joints were stiff, and this had been a hard trek for a man his age. Another night sleeping outdoors, on the hard ground, would not help. They had meagre supplies between them. I guessed they had set off straight from Crag. Fider must have predicted where we would go.

"I know not if you have been ill-used, or if you used me," Beck said. "I give you another chance: speak. Tell us what you know of the weapon, of the attack on Crag, of Mondegreen's future plans. Tell us if he killed both the Syld and Tarklow, and how he escaped from the pinnacle to do it. Or... tell us if you killed them. I knew revenge motivated you, but I did not see a murderous instinct behind your eyes. Tell me now if I was wrong."

I did not speak.

He gave up, and preparations began for the night.

* * *

A NIGHT BIRD was hunting, skimming the weeds with its sharp vision for small animals. It gave out soft screeches, now and then. The fire had died down to a quiet glow, and I was too far away for any warmth to reach me. They had offered to lie me down closer to the stone slab, but I shook my head violently, and eventually they had left me alone.

They slept in a circle around the fire, but I felt no desire to close my own eyes. I scanned the night, looked for something. A camera, whatever that was. The collar of a white shirt, turned up high. A silver coin, suddenly heavy in my pocket. Something.

The screech of the bird was a sharp, rusty sound, like the turn of a key in an old lock.

My stomach grumbled. I had been fed some apple by the man, Tredd, cutting it up and slipping it into my mouth with impartial efficiency. But it was not enough. My watchfulness demanded energy. I could have fallen upon a full meal, devoured it easily.

"I have this," murmured Starke. She had been out walking a perimeter, keeping moving—no doubt to stave off sleep—but now she returned, and sat beside me. She opened the pouch at her waist, took out something small and flat, broke it in two. She placed one half in my mouth. A biscuit! A biscuit from Crag's kitchens, one of the kind they used to make for guards on long shifts. They could keep long, were baked twice. I sucked it until it dissolved into sugary sand on my tongue.

She pocketed the other half. "I am a soft touch," she said, shaking her head. But I had seen her in action; *soft* was not how I would have described her. "Well, maybe a soft touch for you, knowing how Tommo liked you. He told me so. He said there was strength in you, and he admired that."

The bird called out again. I heard a sound like the rustling of leaves close by; perhaps it had swooped, and found its target.

"You have lost your love," she said, quietly. She drew closer to my ear. "I, too, have lost my love. I saw his body." She pulled up her knees, hugged them to her chest. "When they broke down the gate I saw him, still standing. The last one standing. He fell backwards as it came down, and they surged forwards, as one. They trampled him. They are animals, the north. How could you give yourself to one of them, to their ways?"

Across the fire someone shifted, but I thought it a movement of sleep, still. Starke hesitated, then went on, "We were overrun, even Beck shrank back, and Fider called, 'This way, this way.' He took us to a hole in the gardening patch and we crawled from Crag, a handful of us. We found the beach. We could not have been more than an hour behind you. I hated you, then, for having your love while mine lay broken to pieces. But today I saw him step off into the chasm, away from you. He left you alone to face us. He was not worthy of your love. I think perhaps I was not worthy of Tommo's. He said, 'Come with me, be a farmer, I know the land before the fire turns too hot, in the east.' I told him we would not survive, I cried, he comforted me. Then he died. He died and I did not believe in us. Mondegreen did not believe in you enough to stay with you. I don't think he will return."

She did not think Mondegreen dead.

I ran it over and over in my mind: what I had seen, how we had all been looking the other way. He had simply vanished. Was he not the great Mondegreen?

She was wrong about one thing: I had never been in love with Mondegreen. Admiration, gratitude, yes. Obsession for his stories, his way of telling, and jealousy of his gifts, yes. None of these words should be confused with love.

She murmured on about Tommo, and the life that might have come if she had been a better person—one who had given him courage before the arrival of the enemy, rather than taking it from him. I envied her the certainty of that one moment she should have handled differently. I could not say the same myself.

IMBERLEY CAME STRAIGHT to me upon taking over the watch. She looked me over for injuries, her hands gentle, and took out some salve from her own pouch. She rubbed it into my wrists, where the rope burned.

"A wrap of hot pepper you don't get out of this alive," she said. Then she moved away, standing by the chasm. I guessed she waited a while for Starke to fall asleep before she returned, and put her arms around me like a clamp. "You should have talked to me," she muttered. "I would have told you no good would come of trusting a man. Let me find a story that will save you from execution. Say he put his glamour on you. Say you know now he is a monster, and you know where he has gone." She sobbed, which surprised me. All her laconic distance was gone. Perhaps it had always been a performance, the betting and the smart remarks, and she would have let me see the reality if I had confided in her. But it occurred to me that she was only being caring now because she thought they would execute me for the fall of Crag, so nobody would be left to attest to her vulnerability. I was a sure bet. Imberley always had played the odds.

After a while she gave up on me, turned her back, and faced the fire instead. I watched her shoulders shake as she cried, making barely a sound.

BECK WAS A different matter.

He did not come in a cloak of friendship or concern. He took over his shift and fed the fire, placing logs quietly, methodically. Someone coughed. Then all settled down to steady sleep once more and he moved to me, leaned over me once more. His face was hidden from me by the night, and the flames behind him, leaving him in shadow.

"I'd imagine the plan was to throw yourself in too," Beck

said. "Some sort of grand gesture, perhaps, in keeping with the showman. I know the difference between bravery and cowardice. Fider tells me you are no coward, and no idiot either, which is as I thought. But then, Fider says many things that..." His deep voice petered out. "I suppose I have become a coward now, and I will stand beside you for that. I should have stayed at Crag until the end. I have pushed on and on to find you under cover of bringing you to justice, but in my heart I have only been trying to leave the memory of Crag's fall behind. I thank you for not jumping in the chasm. Your cowardice matches my own. And so we will face retribution together." He patted my shoulder. "We can call it our shared fate. Fate is a foolish comfort."

That old expression. I did not make the expected reply: *Good deeds line the finest beds.* What did it mean, anyway? It was nonsense, meant to bring people to a sense of common understanding that they did not possess. Words, words, words.

"But perhaps Tarklow was right, after all," he mused. "He used to say there are no such things as mistakes, and isn't that another way of admitting we can't escape our fate? If we are cowards, the world has finally brought us to that inevitability. I think the world gets worse daily, and we are worsened with it."

Beck left me then, and spent the rest of his watch standing on a small rise above the camp, as tall and straight as ever.

*　　*　　*

WHEN TREDD CAME to his shift he woke slowly and did not speak to me, and for that I was grateful. I thought his silence companionable, at first. Then I thought he hated me, and I feared he would rise suddenly and come at me, or raise his rifle and fire it into my heart without warning. I felt a new respect for those I had once guarded, who had not known my integrity and had spent their hours in horror that I might be a monster. When the one who keeps you prisoner is unknown to you, every kind of possibility occurs to you; it is the terror that makes you pliant, not guilt.

Only when Tredd's head lolled back, coming to rest on the remains of the wall where he'd chosen to sit, did I realise he had fallen back to sleep.

A dereliction of duty. Beck would make him pay if he found out. I shook my head in disapproval.

One of the figures closest to the fire shifted, worked their way towards me in a crawl, moving very slowly. I watched for long minutes, wondering what Fider felt he had to say to me now, when he had once wanted to never speak to me again.

He finally arrived, out of breath with his crawling, and squeezed my hands between his own, rubbing them a little. "You are cold," he whispered, and took off his cloak, throwing it over my shoulders. He rummaged in his own pouch and I hoped for more food, but he produced a small knife, of all things, and began to saw at the rope around my wrists. The rasp of the blade on the fibre of the rope could not have been loud, but it filled my ears. Surely someone would wake.

"You and I both know he is not dead," Fider breathed. "He has been taken up by his kind, they come and go through the air somehow, I am researching this. I will get the others to listen. I will not stop until they understand this threat. He said he would rid this world of them all, and perhaps he has done as he promised. But we must make sure. Go. Find out if others remain. Gather knowledge. I will stay here, try to lead them away from you. Tell them he taught you a trick or two. You are younger, you have energy, I am too old, too old for this fight."

The rope gave, then slithered away from my wrists and fell to the ground.

I stood. Everything hurt. Every muscle was cold, and stiff, and I would not be stopped, I made for the chasm, I strode to its edge. I did not stumble, or make a sound. My toes crested the lip. I looked down, and down. I peered far into the black. Was it grainy? Was it a fine sand that could be pushed through, to emerge, to emerge—

Beck was right. I was a coward.

The extent of the drop overtook me: I swayed; I fell back. I turned. Fider was there, his hands pressed over his mouth. Such fear. All was fear. I ran along the edge of the chasm, then angled towards the Mutuality, certain someone would call out behind me. There was the one standing wall of the building that had been my home, jutting up, and I thought of trying to find a place to hide there, but I went on to the bridge that still stood, where the mouth of the river could be crossed.

Upon it stood a woman.

She waited at the crest, looking over the sea, in rich clothes: a long cloak, with a voluminous hood pulled over her head, shielding her face from view. The way she touched the low wall with gloved hands made me think of the Allynx Syld, all grace, always the right look to her. How many would be at the perfect place in the perfect moment? It had to be her. I found a burst of energy and ran to her, but as soon as I drew near I realised my mistake. This was not the Syld. I knew it before she threw back her hood and looked at me. This woman was older, with an unremarkable face and an amiable smile of greeting for me. I stopped in my tracks, but her smile did not falter.

"Come on," she said. "I have a place you can hide."

She led me from the bridge, down a side street that ended in an impassable mound of brick, but no, it hid a sharp turn to a broken wall, and within it, low to the ground, a hole that could be squeezed through.

"Please," she said. She stood back. I got down on my hands and knees, feeling the rough stones dig into my palms and knees. The dust tickled my nose. I felt my way forward, inched along, blind. Something sharp grazed my back and I recoiled, tried to stay low. It came to me that the ground was sloping away from me. The pebbles I dislodged trickled downwards. This was a tunnel, leading under the earth.

Then I felt cold metal, tubular—a pipe, vertical, and another, horizontal. They were joined together to form a crossbar. There were more. A ladder, it was a ladder, I swung myself around to the rungs and started down, not far. There was a sudden light, beneath me, and an open space. The air was less dusty. Two more rungs, and I felt solid floor under my feet.

"Move back," called the woman, above me, and she descended the final rungs. My eyes began to adjust to the light, and I saw the large room around us, with curved brick walls. The light came from lanterns resting on the floor, unlike any I had seen: balls of a glass that looked frosty although the room was warm. I could see no oil or wick, and they burned very steadily. The glow was strong.

"They are powered by the sun," said the woman. "I take them out during the day, let them soak up the rays, and they keep the basement lit. Nobody will find you here. You're safe." She took off her cloak and hung it on a peg by the ladder, which leaned against a partial collapse where I guessed stairs had once stood.

I knew this room. It was familiar to me: not within my own memory, but from Mondegreen. I looked over the large crates, and the strange pieces of metal and smooth black material collected in heaps. I knew this was what Mondegreen would have called *technology*, holding the secrets to the other world. And there: a circle of this new machinery, with ropes snaking from its centre. A centre filled with black sand.

The woman said, "I'm not keeping you against your will: you're free to go any time, I promise you. But you are welcome to stay until they stop searching for you, if you would like. I only ask that you might listen, as I have things I would say. What do you say?"

There was no energy left in me, and no voice with which to argue.

I sat with my back against the closest crate, and shut my eyes. I wanted to be close to the portal, to what it represented. Escape. I saw the body of Tarklow, next to the dying form of the Syld. I saw Beck's face, calling on Mondegreen to *hold*. I saw Crag destroyed, Droad in pieces. I opened my eyes again, and nodded.

She had water, and bread, and eels from the river that had been fried and cooled. She brought them to me, and said,

BOOK FOUR
COLLISION

To THE EAST there are vast plains of hard land, baked by a heat that sinks deep into the soil until all turns to fire, and one can go no further.

To the west there are the dunes of the cold desert, where Frietown stands like a stalagmite, and beyond that only the endless ice sands that shift with the biting wind. There is no way to chart a course, and one must turn back or be lost.

To the south there are the waves. They lap the coast with a deceptive meekness, but one need only sail for half a day to see the waves leap tall, take on a determination to bring down even the hardiest of boats. The waves claim everyone who ventures too far across the surface of its secrets.

To the north there are the great mountains of this world. One can stand very small before them, but to climb them leads only to air too thin to breathe, and a blinding light that, if followed, leads nowhere.

My name is Gwen Last. I come from one of the three great families of the far north.

We of the far north know how to live on the edge of this world. There are caves in the mountains, deep holes into warm burrows, and long networks of tunnels that have never been revealed to outsiders. There are animals, too. Not the ferocious allynx—that was an invention of our own to keep the curious away. But there are deer that graze on the dark mosses that dot the lower valleys, and small hares, hard to catch, and osters in the streams, long and clever and wiry. There's no taste like them. Life is hard, in the north, but we have a secret, and we have good reason not to reveal it.

This world is a box. It cannot be escaped. It has four sides, unbroachable, impassable. We are sealed within it. We live one way, we speak one language. It is the language of a small part of the world without our own. There, people speak many languages and have many thoughts. Their world is not a box. It is a vast globe. If one travels to the cold white edge of land, one emerges back to green. If one sails for months into endless blue, one returns to the land that was left behind. There is more of everything. More colour, more sound, more beauty and more ugliness. There are ways to love and hate that cannot be imagined.

We of the far north know this, and many things more. We have the memory of ages. Nothing is forgotten. We are trained from infanthood for this, and to receive a certain knowledge: In the depths of the caves are three small holes, each guarded by a family, and through these holes one can travel to an island on the other world. We have done this for many generations. We can settle on either side, and I chose to live there, for a while. I fell in love, and formed a tiny family of my own.

Before that: I remember the first time I stepped through into the other world. I found myself within a room of a grand house, on a stretch of moorland. My brother and sister were waiting for me. They were older, and had passed through the year before. They welcomed me, and showed me wondrous things. Instant knowledge, speed, power. All the people of the north had an equal stake in the riches we made. I travelled around the world over and over, never ceasing to find amazement in the way one language, one landscape, changed to another. I met my husband in a southern continent. He served me food, and asked me if I wished to see historical sights. I asked if he would take me himself, and he laughed, and said he knew nothing of the past, and I loved him.

Then my family contacted me. They told me that a way had been found to open more holes, and I made it my mission to find out more. I started work in the company that owned the knowledge—one of the many faces used by the far north to protect its information. That company was called Collision.

It was my brother and sister who suggested we make a game of it. Something that is a game is never taken seriously. It is a diversion down a long road of hope and illusion, while the real path lies untrodden. It is a technique we have used often. A man called Trevor Arklow was found, and set up in business in a city called Portsmouth. My family agreed he reminded us of an oster, and so it was. We let him take on workers, and shape games from the box that we sprang from. He dealt with my brother and sister, and I joined later, and watched. I watched until I realised that nothing good could come of these flashy tricks and bold statements of chance. I talked to my brother and sister, and saw they had grand plans in place that I could not condone. The small world is encased within the large, that is true, but I was not ready to make the small a plaything. They sought money and power for its own end, and had employed people who wanted the same thing.

We argued.

It is a strange thing to remember every conversation, every look, and see them all as one error after the other. But one cannot see direction until one has arrived, and can look back at the road taken. I had not cultivated good relations with my family, choosing to live with my husband and daughter as if nothing else existed. But the presence of the holes teaches one that where there is existence, there must be acknowledgement. This is why we train to remember all that we can—so that nothing is overlooked, or left to chance.

On the other side of the artificial hole lay Vella Iffluce, a grand building that had belonged to the far north for hundreds of years, unbeknownst to the south, or indeed, to the leaders of the north, who were not of interest to us. I travelled there and appealed directly to my elders. They had faith in my siblings, not in me. They ordered me back to the north, and I obeyed.

Why do we obey commands?

I felt the weight of history, a history of compliance, upon me. I believed in the goodness that comes from order. I do not know if this is a product of this world or the other. I think we want to imagine our lives as a certain kind of suffering that comes with experience, and that includes thinking there is a purpose to absence: through disappearance, through death. Each story increases an understanding of what has been lost, and why we learn—and who does not want to be part of such stories?

I will not believe my family brought about the destruction of Droad. But it is fair to say that something went wrong. Something was overlooked. I heard of the weapon, I knew how it was caused. I do not know why. My mother was in Vella Iffluce when Droad fell. I came back to the outskirts of the city, but did not dare to step inside for a long time, knowing all that the weapon may do over time. But this world is a box: how long before a poison spreads through all parts of such a shape? I supposed it made little difference, one mile or two. I returned here, found this place.

Here is the gamble: does the portal still work?

If I try to enter and find a dead world on the other side, I must mourn, and that will be the end of me.

If I leave this place, then I give up my opportunity for revenge, for redemption. For understanding.

So here I stay.

I have unstoppable, endlessly churning memories. The moments of my life. Failures. One might say—why dwell on failures? Isn't every moment of success sharp in your mind, too? And I say to that—one must exist within the other. North and south, east and west, flat and round, dull and sharp: these are not equals. One is always bigger. One swallows, and the other is digested. Failure eats success. The other world has eaten ours, and had its fill.

I heard your voices, and then I saw you last night. I saw Miles, and knew him. I followed you both. I should have approached you. I heard him ask you for stories, and I would say the same. Tell your story, whatever happens next. But remember to say that this world is a free one, free from responsibility, free from shame. It was never what it seemed to be, but then, nothing is, nothing ever has been. I can say this with confidence, and now I will say no more.

BOOK FIVE
COLLUSION

CHAPTER TWENTY-SIX

I SLEPT.

When I woke I had no idea how much time had passed. I was refreshed, clear-headed in a way I had not been in weeks. I felt a new space in my mind where I could make decisions. Mondegreen's spell was broken. The weight of his words was lifted. What had the woman said? That I should be free from responsibility? It was a comfort to me. I wished I could thank her, but she was gone. I had a feeling I would not have known her again if she passed me on a busy street.

Could I believe her? Was he dead?

I did not have to make a decision one way or another. Not yet.

I examined the portal, wondered if he awaited me on the other side. If I could become part of the shitshow: the cafés and the jobs and the magic tricks and the shouting and the island

and the continent and the weapon and science and business and training montages and television and all the other words he had used. Change. I could become change.

I wanted that.

Revenge was not in this world, not for me, not any longer. Whoever had been responsible for the death of my mother, the destruction of the city, was long gone. A world away. I had to find change. A different story. I steeled myself, I curled my hand into a fist, I plunged it into the black sand at the centre of the portal, and

CHAPTER TWENTY-SEVEN

and my hand vanished into the sand. It felt no different. I could not see it, but I could feel it, cool and whole, so I crawled forward, I shut my eyes, I felt the sand fall over my face, my body, and I emerged, and dared to open my eyes upon another world.

The space was cavernous, yet brightly lit, free from shadow. I could not tell where the light came from. All surfaces were dull metal, including containers that had been stacked in piles in all corners. Some of them had square black eyes set within them. Snaking ropes crossed the floor and ran between my hands and knees, into the portal.

I got up and ran my hands through my hair, over my clothes, thinking to find them covered in sand. There was nothing. Even so, I felt weighed down, gritty, as if it had found its way into my boots and pockets, and more than that, swallowed into my body although I had kept my mouth tightly shut throughout.

High above, I spotted a rail running along the length of the vast room. A platform, perhaps? I gazed up at it, expecting someone to be there. An architect, a mastermind. A person of power. Someone who could explain all this to me.

Mondegreen. I waited for Mondegreen.

I stood for as long as I could bear his absence.

This is a box too, I thought. *I am in a new kind of box. And boxes built to keep people within must have airholes.*

There was a door ahead of me.

The door was ajar.

Every step toward it was an achievement: the bravest action I've ever taken. The lights were beyond bright, beating down upon me with great force, and each footstep echoed like a drum. I dreaded to find what lay beyond the door. A dead world, a disintegrated pile of dreams? Poison. Poison. I reached the door. It was made of the same cool metal as the room, the containers, the portal. I risked a glance behind me. Yes, the portal still stood. I could drag myself back, if I had to.

I pushed the door fully open.

A tall young man with deep, unfocused eyes faced me. He was not quick, I'd wager, but he was big. I thought perhaps I could have outrun him if I had not felt so heavy in myself. He wore one silver garment—trousers and shirt joined at the waist—that led up to a high neck and down to thick-soled boots. He held a thin piece of wood with blank pieces of paper upon it.

The time for my silence was over. Gwen's words compelled me. I had to tell some sort of story, and make account of my appearance here, out of my own time and place. But I could not think of what to say, and he did not seem to care one way or another. I was, apparently, not even of enough interest to make him stir.

I realised he was not looking at me, even though his eyes aligned with mine. He did not see me. I lifted my hands, waved them before his face. I moved closer, as close as I dared. He had a small mark beside his nose, a reddening of the skin there. A pimple. He was very young, and perhaps ill. He sweated. But his eyelashes were very long, and strong, and beautiful. I wanted him to see me. The clothing he wore was bunched at the underarm, as if it was too small. I thought to touch the creases, radiating out from where his arm met his shoulder.

No, I would not touch him. His ignorance of me was complete.

I had played the role of the invisible watcher before. I knew it well. I understood it.

So I left him behind, the strange guard, and I explored the boat upon which the portal stood. I found the suite, empty, and the rooms, quiet. Everyone subdued. They murmured in low voices, and not one of them saw me.

I tired of them. I made my way to the nearby island, remembering Mondegreen's childhood, and searched out Cosham. One thing was certain: no destruction had been wreaked upon it. It stands still, stands firm. On it goes, and I with it. It reinvents itself daily, and yet the heaviness of it does not change. It is like a thick cloak that one wears, the fur of a monster one has slain. A trophy and a reminder: this is the reality of what has been made by my actions.

What a magnificent world this is. I would not think of leaving it.

In Cosham I went from house to house, staring through windows into the homes of people who all watched the small boxes that contained other realities, as if that could ever match up to their own possibilities upon which they did not act. The people were agog. It took time to find two such people who bore the image of Mondegreen, in a frame, above their fireplace.

I slipped into their lives and sat with them: the parents of the legend, the hero. My saviour. I sat at their feet. They often spoke of him, and wondered where he was. They said: *He used to like this programme*, or *Remember how he loved beans on toast, when he was little?* They both knew him well and did not know him at all, and in that way we were quite alike, and we missed him, the three of us, equally, for a while.

Then I moved on. There is room to do that, here.

CHAPTER TWENTY-SEVEN

and my hand vanished into the sand. It felt no different. I could
not see it, but I could feel it, cool and whole, so I crawled forward,
I shut my eyes, I felt the sand fall over my face, my body, and I
emerged, and dared to open my eyes upon another world.

A beach, at night, with the light of a full moon broken
to bits on the playful waves, all the way to a deep horizon.
Fine white sand under my hands and feet. A little boat was
moored to a small jetty, not far away, and beyond that were
rocks becoming boulders, growing, changing to hills, then
distant mountains, glorious, austere. The air was very good,
sweet with horseplant. I spotted its prickly demeanour dotted
between the rocks, and I stood, knowing which world I planted
my feet upon. This was home. Although I did not know this
beach, I was home.

I spotted a tower, further down the coastline, and walked to it, feeling light, wondering if my feet sank into the sand at all. The tower was quite plain, conical. Made of a pale stone. Not that tall, and with only one window, set high under the pointed roof. I approached, and he leaned out, and called down to me. "Finally!" he said.

His white shirt fit his shoulders well, and it looked very clean. His hair was tied back from his face. I could not think, could not breathe, for happiness. He looked at me, and I at him.

"Come, come," he said. "Don't let Archie see you so. This is a light world, not a heavy one, so make light for the sake of the three of us, together, as we should always have been. Smile, Elize. Smile."

The Syld squeezed in beside him at the window, and gazed down with open friendliness that warmed me utterly. "Smiles are like sleight of hand," she said. Her fur stood proud from her shoulders. "Neither should be performed for the sake of those who can't appreciate the effort involved."

Mondegreen raised an eyebrow at me.

I called up, "Well then, I am happy to smile for you both, for you understand exactly what it costs me to make my expression set so, and I know what price you pay when you return it." The words flowed easily from me. We smiled. They threw over a silken ladder so fine it could barely be seen, and held it in place while I climbed, and when it was pulled back up we were safe, and complete.

"Well, what now?" said Mondegreen.

"A story!" said the Syld. She sat on the comfortable bed, and patted either side of her. We took our places. "Tell a story. Fill it with tricks and fights and chases and journeys across land and sea. And make it a tale of magic, I pray. Some people cannot stand such fantasies, but I am a lover of the incredulous and the impossible, and nothing combines those things so well as magic."

"Very well," he said. "Whenever you are ready, Elize."

They waited for me to start talking.

It was all I had ever wanted.

I opened my mouth, and found myself saying:

We were called to the dock to collect a box.

CHAPTER TWENTY-SEVEN

and my hand went straight through. The grainy effect of the darkness was not solid, but some sort of residual illusion. This looked like a hole that could lead to exciting places, but it was only a dead end.

There was to be no escape this way.

I waited for a while, picking through the crates. I found metal contraptions and more material similar to the lamps, hard and black. None of them seemed to do anything useful. Tarklow had spent years looking for such things, sending soldiers into Droad to cart back box after box. I stood amongst his treasure, and found nothing there to admire. I thought of taking one of the items as proof of the other world, but the idea seemed ridiculous to me, and I did not want to carry Droad anymore. When it became clear that the woman would not return I climbed the ladder, and found a new morning outside, just on the cusp of tipping into midday. I must have slept through the day and the night, and I guessed Beck and his soldiers would be long gone, chasing shadows back to the north.

Seabirds were wheeling overhead, calling. I looked up into the blue sky for them, and headed back to the bridge. The birds were diving into the shallow point of the rivermouth, emerging with bright flashes in their beaks. Eels. The best in the land. Everyone knew it.

I climbed over the bridge and dropped down into the water to stand waist deep. The birds took fright, left me to my own company, but the eels were swarming and had no fear. They were a great gift in the smallest of worlds. I tried to catch them, but no, they were far too quick for me. I laughed for each one that escaped me. They were all swimming in the same direction, out to sea. No matter what happened they swam this way in the morning, and were gone by the afternoon. I felt sudden warmth on my face, wetness; I lifted my hand, and found my fingers stained with blood. A nosebleed. I plunged into the water, submerged myself fully. Nothing but eels, all too slippery to hold, swimming in the ribbons of my blood, and it was time to emerge again, anew, accepting my responsibility for this beautiful world around me. One life was over. Another was about to begin.

*   *   *

AND THERE IT is: the story that I owed you in payment for a little food, and a bed for the night in these terrible times. I give you a choice as to how it ends. Would you care to wager on a truth? No? Well, you are wise to stay clear of such games. The world worsens daily. A wise man once said that to me.

Fate is a foolish comfort, but I will believe in it for as long as I can.

I hope you enjoyed the tale. I had very fine teachers.

ACKNOWLEDGEMENTS

It's true. When it comes to telling tales, I have had some very fine teachers.

Thank you to David Ian Rabey for starting me down the path, and being so generous and wise throughout this journey.

Max Edwards gives so much energy to my stories, and is determined to see them out in the world. Thanks Max.

Thank you to everyone at Solaris for bringing so much effort and skill to turning this tale into a book. David Thomas Moore, my wonderful editor, understands many stories including this one, and helps them to become all they should be. Sophie Clark, my proofreader, caught several things I should have spotted, for which I'm fervently grateful. Dominic Forbes designed the wonderful cover, and Natalie Charlesworth and Jess Gofton plotted and organised and got that cover splashed in all the right places. I'm very grateful for all your expertise.

This book is dedicated to Tim Stretton, who is a great writer and a lover of classic fantasy tales. He reads all my books first and tells me what I need to fix before I'll risk another person seeing them. Tim, *The Misheard World* owes you a debt.

It also owes a debt to the people who are with me daily, from fellow writers online to my close family and friends, who have learned to repeat every conversation because I'm usually off in some fantasy land. Apologies, and love, and thanks, thanks, thanks.

FIND US ONLINE!

www.rebellionpublishing.com

/solarisbooks   /solarisbks

/solarisbooks   /solarisbooks.
bsky.social

SIGN UP TO OUR NEWSLETTER!

rebellionpublishing.com/newsletter

YOUR REVIEWS MATTER!

Enjoy this book? Got something to say?

Leave a review on Amazon, GoodReads or with your
favourite bookseller and let the world know!

Arthur C. Clarke Award Nominated Author

ALIYA WHITELEY

THE BEAUTY

TENTH ANNIVERSARY EDITION

⊙ SOLARISBOOKS.COM

Arthur C. Clarke Award Nominated Author

"Brilliant in
its playful
inventiveness."
The FT

ALIYA WHITELEY

THREE EIGHT ONE

"Wonderfully
alienating."
★ ★ ★ ★ ★
SFX

SOMETIMES WE LOSE OUR WAY TO FIND IT